W9-CQL-644

"Twenty Thousand Dollars."

It was the man at the back. He'd called out what would undoubtedly be the closing bid. And as he spoke, he stepped forward, out of the shadows.

He was dressed in a tux that looked as if it had been made for his tall, lean frame. He wore his hair close-cropped, whereas the last time she'd seen him it had been long and ragged. Still she recognized him immediately. Not just because his image occasionally graced the pages of magazines.

No matter how he was dressed or what he'd done to his hair, she'd know Matt Ballard anywhere.

Dear Reader,

I've always had a soft spot for geeky guys. Maybe it's because my husband is a computer programmer. Whenever I blog on JauntyQuills.com, I even refer to him as The Geek. My favorite character in *Sixteen Candles* is Anthony Michael Hall's. I mean, sure Jake Ryan was hot and studly, but Anthony Michael Hall was funnier, kinder and had way better lines. And out of all of Suzanne Brockmann's fabulous heroes, Ken Karmody is my favorite. A coincidence? I think not.

In my experience, most of those guys who are geeky and overlooked in high school grow up to be funny, clever, hardworking men who are completely devoted to the women they love. That's the perfect hero right there.

For Matt Ballard, I aimed to tell just such a story. I loved both him and Claire. I hope you do too!

Emily McKay

EMILY McKAY

THE BILLIONAIRE'S BRIDAL BID

Published by Silhouette Books

America's Publisher of Contemporary Romance

If you purchased this book without a cover you should be aware
that this book is stolen property. It was reported as "unsold and
destroyed" to the publisher, and neither the author nor the
publisher has received any payment for this "stripped book."

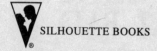

SILHOUETTE BOOKS

ISBN-13: 978-0-373-73064-3

THE BILLIONAIRE'S BRIDAL BID

Recycling programs
for this product may
not exist in your area.

Copyright © 2010 by Emily McKaskle

All rights reserved. Except for use in any review, the reproduction
or utilization of this work in whole or in part in any form by any
electronic, mechanical or other means, now known or hereafter
invented, including xerography, photocopying and recording, or in
any information storage or retrieval system, is forbidden without
the written permission of the editorial office, Silhouette Books,
233 Broadway, New York, NY 10279 U.S.A.

This is a work of fiction. Names, characters, places and incidents are
either the product of the author's imagination or are used fictitiously, and
any resemblance to actual persons, living or dead, business establishments,
events or locales is entirely coincidental.

This edition published by arrangement with Harlequin Books S.A.

For questions and comments about the quality of this book please contact us
at Customer_eCare@Harlequin.ca.

® and TM are trademarks of Harlequin Books S.A., used under license.
Trademarks indicated with ® are registered in the United States Patent
and Trademark Office, the Canadian Trade Marks Office and in other
countries.

Visit Silhouette Books at www.eHarlequin.com

Printed in U.S.A.

EMILY McKAY

has been reading romance novels since she was eleven years old. Her first Harlequin Romance came free in a box of Hefty garbage bags. She has been reading and loving romance novels ever since. She lives in Texas with her geeky husband, two kids and too many pets. Her debut novel, *Baby, Be Mine,* was a RITA® Award finalist for Best First Book and Best Short Contemporary. She was also a 2009 *RT Book Reviews* Career Achievement nominee for Series Romance. To learn more, visit her website at www.EmilyMcKay.com.

For my father, who has always supported me,
even when he didn't quite understand my love of
romance novels and I didn't quite understand physics...
and who first taught me to appreciate smart, funny men.

One

"Rumor has it, you've agreed to be one of the bachelorettes in the auction this weekend."

Claire Caldiera looked up from pouring coffee for Rudy Windon, one of the old-timers who frequented her diner, to see Victor Ballard leering at her with one elbow propped on the counter. Suppressing an eye-roll—she *so* did not need to waste time fending off Vic's advances this morning—she pulled the rag from the waistband of her apron and swiped at the counter near Rudy's coffee cup.

"You need anything else, Rudy, you ask, okay?" She smiled warmly at the aging farmer and school board member.

"Nah, honey, I'll be fine here with my doughnut."

Nodding, she carried the pot back to the coffeemaker and slid it onto the warmer. Vic propelled himself away from the counter and followed her down to the end.

In the small town where they'd both grown up and now lived, Vic fancied himself a great catch. Too bad she knew he was a slimeball.

"Is it a rumor or am I finally going to get a chance to take you out on the town?" Vic asked.

She turned to face Vic, scanning her restaurant, Cutie Pies, for a distraction. Unfortunately, the half dozen customers she had midmorning were contentedly munching away on their meals. She forced a smile. "It's true. I'll be up on the auction block tomorrow night."

Vic's face spilt in a slow smile that would have had half the women in town fanning themselves. The problem was, she was part of the half of the population that was tired of his slick good looks. Vic may have the lantern jaw of a superhero and the clear blue eyes of a choirboy, but his practiced charm made her stomach churn.

"Good thing I've been saving up my change then," he murmured.

"I guess."

As if he'd need to save up money for anything. Vic came from one of the richest families in their small town of Palo Verde, California. But that was the least of her complaints about Vic.

The real reason she'd never voluntarily go on a date with Vic Ballard was the he reminded her too much of his brother, Matt. Matt had all of Vic's good looks and none of the dissipation. To her, Matt was infinitely more appealing. Or rather, he had been back when she was young and stupid. For six brief weeks when she was eighteen, Matt had made her believe a guy like him could really love someone like her. He'd convinced her that the kind of fairy-tale love she'd always dreamed of was possible. She'd never forgive him for that.

Vic Ballard was merely a creep, but it was Matt who had broken her heart.

She considered herself lucky that it was Vic who wandered through her diner at least once a day, whereas Matt never returned to Palo Verde. He hated the small town in which they'd all grown up almost as much as she suspected he hated her. Since their breakup, Matt had gone on to be one of the founders and the current chief technology officer of FMJ Inc., a hugely successful company based in the Bay Area.

Matt and his high school buddies Ford Langley and Jonathon Bagdon had formed the company while they were still in college. Even before FMJ was officially incorporated, they had a long history of pooling their resources in profitable ventures. All of which had made Matt a very rich man—and even more out of her league than he had been when they were in high school. Back then, he'd merely been the second son of the town's wealthiest family to her poor white trash.

"So then the rumors are true?" Vic was saying. "You're finally breaking your no-dating rule?"

"What can I say?" She forced a smile. "It's for a good cause."

The Palo Verde Benevolent Society was hosting a huge gala to raise money to stock the children's section of the new library. Bachelorette auction fundraisers were more the domain of sparkling debutantes than of hardworking business owners like her. She knew she was out of her league. But when one of the slated bachelorettes broke her leg at the last minute and had to drop out, the Benevolent Society had talked Claire into stepping up and filling the gap. How could she say no when she'd spent so much of her own troubled youth in the sanctuary of the previous library? It was a cause dear to her heart, even if it meant she'd have to suffer through an evening with a jerk like Vic Ballard.

Why he'd even want to bid on her, she didn't know. Vic had ruined her sister's life. He couldn't seriously believe she was interested in him. Of course, that hadn't stopped him from hitting on her repeatedly over the years. In fact, he was the reason she'd instituted the blanket no-dating rule. But apparently his ego knew no bounds. Besides, it could be worse. It could be Matt Ballard threatening to bid on her instead of Vic. Then she'd really be in trouble.

If she had to choose between philandering jerks, she'd gladly choose the one who wasn't her first love.

"You're bidding a thousand dollars for…what is that? Muffins?" The woman's voice came from just over Matt's shoulder. "For someone who didn't want to come tonight, you're sure spending a lot on muffins."

Matt finished writing his paddle number on the silent auction form and straightened before turning around. After all, the sardonic purr of Kitty Biedermann's voice was one he was familiar with. Earlier that year, FMJ had bought up Kitty's company, Biedermann Jewelry. FMJ usually specialized in buying out tech companies, rather than chains of jewelry stores. But the decision to branch out had been profitable for FMJ. As an added bonus, Ford had fallen hard for the sultry Kitty. Matt couldn't blame him.

As always, she looked gorgeous. Dressed in a crimson cocktail dress that could have been painted on, with her hair an artful tumble around her shoulders, she outshone every woman there. He gave her a buss on the cheek. "They're good muffins," he said.

She returned his smile, layering on the flirtation. "I bet they are."

Kitty was a hell of woman. He might just be tempted to hit on her, if she wasn't already married to one of his best friends. "So when are you going to ditch Ford and run away with me?"

Her gaze shifted to the bar on the far side of the patio where Ford stood in line waiting for drinks. The country club patio overlooked the verdant golf course and the rolling foothills of the Sierra Nevada Mountains beyond.

Looking over at her husband now, for an instant Kitty's eyes held a love so compelling, it made Matt's chest tighten with some emotion he didn't want to examine too closely. Probably indigestion from being back in this damn town.

Then her expression shifted to mock sympathy. "Oh, you couldn't get a date to drive all the way out here?" She shook her head, clucking in disapproval. "It's all these skinny models you date. Their butts just aren't made for long car rides."

He chuckled, despite his grim mood. "Yeah, it's a real epidemic. Models who are too skinny."

Kitty's lips curved into a sultry smile. "They should have a gala fundraiser for that."

"I'll organize it myself if it means I can get out of this one."

Just then, Ford approached with the drinks and handed Matt an Anchor Steam. "Let me guess. He's trying to sucker you in with all that 'My parents didn't love me enough' garbage."

Matt forced a smirk, tucking the auction paddle into his back pocket as he took the beer from Ford. "Hey, would I try to charm your woman?"

"In a minute."

Before Ford could respond, Matt's mother zeroed in on them.

"There you are, darling! The president of the Benevolent Society has been begging me for an introduction." She spoke with boisterous false cheer as she kissed the air near his cheeks.

"Hello, Mommy dearest," he said drolly.

She frowned, but said nothing. After brief greetings, Ford and Kitty discreetly excused themselves. As soon as the others were out of earshot, his mother moved closer and whispered, "Please don't call me that."

"It's term of affection," he said drily between sips of his beer, suddenly wishing he'd asked Ford to bring him something stronger.

"It isn't. It's an insult. You know I don't like it when you call me that." Her mouth pursed in disapproval. Without the benefit of Botox injections her face would probably be permanently fixed in a scowl.

"And you know I don't like it when you introduce me to your friends like I'm your prize pony."

She leveled a shrewd gaze at him. Finally she nodded. "Very well. No introductions then." She linked her arm through his, preparing to parade around the room with him. Apparently, her no introductions agreement didn't exclude merely showing him off. "I hope you've been bidding generously in the silent auction."

"I know you have."

When she saw his bid, she clucked with disapproval. "Really, Matt. A thousand dollars for muffins is hardly appropriate."

"You're the one who said I should bid generously."

"Now you're being purposefully obtuse."

"I happen to like the muffins from Cutie Pies."

Hanging out at the town diner had been one of the few bright spots of his teenage years.

His mother merely shook her head. "How in the world is Chloe supposed to deliver a muffin to you every day, when you live three hours from here?"

"I'm sure she'll figure it out." He was scanning the room, hoping to find Ford and Kitty again and then quickly extract himself from his mother's tentacles, but they must have already loaded up with plates and headed into the ballroom where the tables and dance floor were set up and where the live auction would take place. Because of his search, it took a moment for his mother's words to finally sink in. "Who? Doesn't Doris Ann still run Cutie Pies?"

Though not particularly interested in town gossip, he had been planning on stopping by in the morning to catch up with the bustling older woman who'd been like the mother he'd wished he had. Generous and kind, despite her gruff exterior.

"No, Doris Ann retired years ago. Her niece took over. Chloe something. Or maybe Clarissa."

When Estelle realized he'd stopped walking, she turned back to him. "Is something wrong, darling?"

He shook his head to clear it. "Claire. Her name is Claire Caldiera." Forcing himself to meet his mother's calculating gaze, he grinned and added a shrug for effect. "She was a couple of years behind me in school."

Seeming to accept his explanation, his mother slipped her hand into his arm once again. "You always did have a mind for details."

Praying his tone didn't convey the depth of his curiosity, he said, "I didn't realize she'd moved back."

The last time he'd seen her, she'd been heading to

New York with dreams of an exciting new life with her boyfriend, Mitch.

She'd known Mitch for exactly seventy-six hours before dumping Matt and hopping on the back of Mitch's motorcycle in search of adventure. No doubt he remembered that fact precisely because he had such a mind for details.

"Oh, yes. Years ago."

His thoughts had been so focused on Claire, he hadn't noticed that his mother had been steering him toward the dining room where the bachelorette auction was about to take place. As he held the door open for her, he forced his attention back to her words.

"...but you know how your brother is. Once his mind is made up, there's no changing it."

"Yes, he is as stubborn as an ass," Matt said drily.

The emcee of the event was already onstage, gushing about all the hard work it had taken to get this event off the ground.

His mother glared at him. "That's not nice."

"It's not meant to be a compliment. What's he being stubborn about this time?" he asked, gently redirecting her attention away from his flaw and toward his brother's.

"This bachelorette thing."

Matt's gaze settled onto the stage to where a row of six elegantly dressed, perfectly coifed women stood right behind the emcee like a parade of beauty contestants. Five of them were blandly lovely and completely unremarkable. The final one was Claire Caldiera.

The sight of her, after all these years, simultaneously sucked the air out his lungs and brought all of his senses into sharp focus. Just in time for him to catch the end of his mother's rant.

"So why he's so determined to bid on this Chloe girl, I'll never know."

"Claire," Matt muttered as a dull pain thudded through his chest.

"Yes, Claire. Chloe. Whoever, the point is…"

But Matt had once again stopped listening to his mother's words. Not only was Claire back in town, but she was here tonight. Right in front of him. Up on the auction block.

So, his competitive, obnoxious ass of a brother was determined to win a date with Claire? Well, he'd have to get through Matt first.

After all, Matt and Claire had unfinished business.

The stage lights shone so brightly on the emcee and the bachelorettes that Claire could barely see into the ballroom. It was a disconcerting experience for someone not used to standing in the spotlight. She wished now that she'd been the first to go instead of the last.

Mostly she just tried not to fidget during the interminable wait while each of the successive women was auctioned off, amid cheerful catcalls and good-natured heckling. By the time her turn came, the audience was getting restless. The low murmur of chatter and the clattering of silverware on dishes had been slowly inching up.

Finally it was her turn to step forward and stand beside the emcee, Rudy Windon.

Holding the microphone down so the audience wouldn't hear him, Rudy leaned in close and whispered, "You look terrified, Claire."

She tried to smile but felt her lips quiver a bit. "What can I say, it's the first time I've sold myself for charity."

He chuckled and gave her shoulder a quick squeeze. "You'll do fine, hon." At the sight of his friendly smile, something inside of her relaxed.

Then he raised the microphone to his mouth and talked to the audience. "Up next, gentlemen, we have local beauty Claire Caldiera." He paused for a faint smattering of applause. He flashed that good-ol'-boy smile of his at the audience. "Now just about everybody in town knows that Claire here has sworn off dating." The audience chuckled. "You want to tell us why you're not giving the men of Palo Verde more of a chance?"

For a second she just stared blankly at the microphone he'd thrust in front of her as potential answers raced through her mind. *I got tired of being called a tease just because I wasn't ready to hop into bed on the first date.* Yeah, that'd go over well. What about: *The women in my family are too fertile for their own good and have rotten taste in men, so I decided not to risk it.* That one would really bring in the bids. And then there was: *Some jerk broke my heart forever ago, and I'm still not quite over it.* That was the one she didn't say aloud even to herself. Pathetic.

Finally she shrugged and smiled in a way she hoped looked playful instead of beleaguered. "I'm up at four most days making those doughnuts you enjoy so much, Rudy. Most men don't want to want to bring their date home by six."

Rudy winced playfully and patted his belly. "There you have it, men. This is your one chance to keep Claire out late."

At the audience's laughter, she relaxed a smidge more. Okay, maybe this wasn't going to be a total disaster.

Rudy winked at her. "Let's start the bidding at five hundred dollars."

She felt the floor wobble beneath her. Five hundred dollars? Surely no man in his right mind would pay five hundred dollars to take her on a date.

Just when she thought she'd have to run off the stage to puke, time sped up again and someone in the audience raised his paddle.

"Five hundred," Rudy said beside her. "Five hundred. Do I have five-fifty?"

Relief flooded her and hot on its heels was curiosity. Who had raised the paddle? Her eyes adjusted to staring out into the dark room and she caught a glimpse of the man holding the paddle. Vic Ballard. No surprise there.

"Do we have five-fifty?" Rudy was still asking. "Going once. Going twice."

Claire sighed, ready to resign herself to an evening of aerobic grope-dodging.

"Going… Five-fifty, to the gentleman in the back."

The bidder in the back had flashed his paddle so quickly Claire hadn't seen more than a flash of white. And with the lights shining in her eyes, she could see only the vague outline of the man's shape. But whoever he was, people in the crowd recognized him and a murmur spread through the room.

"Do we have six hundred? Six hundred?"

Vic, sitting in the front row, was close enough to the stage that Claire could read his expression. He shifted in his seat, looking over his shoulder. When he turned back, his features had been chiseled into pure determination. His paddle went up.

"Six hundred!" Rudy crowed. "How about seven—" But before he could even finish the question, the paddle in the back flashed. "Seven hundred! Eight hundred? Eight."

From there the bidding moved with a rapidity that made her head spin. A thousand. Fifteen hundred. Two thousand. Five thousand.

With each twitch of the paddle the numbers grew. As the bidding spun out of control, a preternatural hush fell over the audience. Soon the gaze of every audience member was bobbing back and forth between Vic and the mysterious bidder at the back of the room. If the bidding war alone didn't make it obvious, the focus of the audience's rapt attention surely did. This wasn't about her at all.

This was about the rivalry between these two men. Some age-old competition was being played out before the entire town. And she'd been nominated as the prize.

That realization made her chest tighten and her breath quicken. She could think of only one person whom Vic considered an adversary.

But it couldn't be Matt. He'd never bid on a date with her. Not ten dollars, let alone ten thousand.

Which was, she now realized, the number Vic had just agreed to.

The pressure in her chest built. Ten thousand dollars. That was so much money. An insane amount.

The bidder at the back must have thought so, too. Because his paddle remained down for an interminable second. And then another. And another.

Beside her, Rudy was babbling. Extolling her virtues, trying to entice the bidder into upping his bid. But the man's paddle stayed down.

"You're going to let her go, son?" Rudy prodded.

If the man responded, she still couldn't see.

Rudy started in again. "Going to Mr. Vic Ballard. For ten-thousand dollars. Going once. Going twice."

"Twenty thousand dollars."

It was the man at the back. He'd called out what would undoubtedly be the closing bid. And as he spoke, he stepped forward, out of the shadows.

He was dressed in a tux that looked as if it had been made for his tall, lean frame. He wore his hair close-cropped, whereas the last time she'd seen him it had been long and ragged. Still she recognized him immediately. Not just because his image occasionally graced the pages of *Us Weekly* and *OK* magazine.

No matter how he was dressed or what he'd done to his hair, she'd know Matt Ballard anywhere.

Two

The morning after the fundraiser, Claire rolled out of bed at four in the morning, contemplating her cowardice.

She'd fled the stage the instant Rudy had banged his gavel, ending the bidding on her date. Quite simply, she'd been unable to face the stunned silence of the crowd. Or their burning curiosity. She'd hurried home, locked the door, unplugged the phone and turned off her cell, ready to bury her head under a pillow like the proverbial ostrich.

Sleep had eluded her, however. For the first time since she'd bought Cutie Pies from her great-aunt Doris Ann, Claire had welcomed getting up at four to make the buttermilk chocolate doughnuts Cutie Pies was known for.

After last night's bidding war between the Ballard brothers, everyone in town would be wondering what was so special about Claire Caldiera that a date with her would bring to a head the lifelong rivalry between Vic and Matt. Some of those inquiring minds would probably stop by the diner in hopes of catching a replay of last night's display. She might as well sell them some doughnuts.

A classic 1950s diner, Cutie Pies sat on Main Street just opposite Luna, the upscale restaurant that had opened up a few years ago. Booths lined the front of the diner, next to the windows looking out onto street. Red Formica tables were scattered throughout, but the real old-timers sat on the leather-topped stools at the bar, where they were closest to the fresh-brewed coffee and they got their eggs mere seconds after they left the griddle. The kitchen in back, where the mixer and ovens were, had a pass-through window, giving Claire a clear view of the front of the diner as she baked.

She'd tuned her radio into the oldies station when she'd first arrived at the diner. Lights from the occasionally passing car flickered through the dining room, but otherwise, she might have been alone in the world. Scraping down the sides of the mixer and humming along to The Shirelles's "Mama Said," she could pretend her life hadn't gone all to hell in the past twenty-four hours.

In fact, she'd nearly convinced herself that what happened the previous night at the fundraiser wasn't that big a deal. It was, after all, only one date. A single evening. With a man she hated.

No, no. That was too severe. She didn't *hate* him.

She just really, really, *really* didn't want to see him again. Was there a word for that?

He was the first man she'd ever trusted with her fragile heart and he'd broken it. He epitomized every bad decision she'd made in her life. Every mistake. Every wrong turn. Every sacrifice. Seeing him just reminded her of a thousand paths she hadn't taken. And honestly, that was just the last thing she needed right now.

She poked listlessly at the doughnut batter with her spatula. She'd been feeling so restless lately. So hemmed in by her choices and her responsibilities. She dipped her finger into the batter and scooped up a glob. Sucking it off her finger, she considered her options.

Option One: Grit her teeth and bear it.

Option Two: Hire a professional hit man to take out Matt Ballard.

Option Three: Go home now, toss a bag of essentials into her aging Toyota along with her anemic pothos ivy, Fred, and leave Palo Verde again. Maybe this time forever.

Sadly, Option Three was looking pretty darn appealing.

It would be an escape from the malaise that had settled over her during the past few months. More to the point, it was a way to avoid this date. Which was kind of ironic, because the bachelorette auction thing was supposed to solve the problem of how restless she'd been feeling. It wasn't supposed to create more problems.

She stuck a different finger into the batter and fished out another bit of batter. It tasted fine. Just…fine. Okay. Bland, bland, bland.

For nearly thirty years, Cutie Pies had been serving the same chocolate doughnuts. They were so…predictable. Feeling twitchy with rebellious impulses, she crossed to the supply pantry, pulled out a jar of cayenne pepper.

The regulars would pitch a fit, come doughnut time,

but it beat the hell out of making a run for it. Which was what she wanted to do.

Running was in her blood. She knew that. Her mother, her father and her sister—they'd all been runners. When life got tough or things got complicated, they just picked up and left. Her father had started the tradition, walking out on his girlfriend and daughters just five days after Claire's younger sister, Courtney, was born. Their mother had followed suit a few years later. Throughout their childhood, she'd periodically disappear for longer and longer stretches. Each time, when Claire had asked her mother why she was leaving them with their grandparents she'd give some pithy response. Like, "Honey, if you love someone, you've got to set her free," or "Sometimes a woman's just got to feel the wind in her hair," or—and this one was Claire's favorite—"Some people are like sharks. They've got to keep moving to stay alive."

Even at eight, Claire had realized how appropriate the analogy was. Sharks weren't evil or mean. It was just in their nature to consume everything in their path. Even their own young.

For a long time after that, it was just Claire and Courtney together against the rest of the world. Yes, they lived with their grandparents, but they counted on only each other. She'd thought it would always be that way. Then at fifteen, Courtney had gone a little crazy. Gotten pregnant, run away from their grandparents' house and gotten into a heap of trouble. Claire had done everything she could to help her younger sister. But in the end, once the baby had been born and safely adopted, Courtney too had run. The last Claire had heard, Courtney lived in Sacramento, less than an hour away, but apparently too far to visit or even call.

Claire promised to herself long ago she'd never be like her mother or sister. She'd never run from her problems. So why was she thinking about it now? Merely because Matt was back in her life? For one measly night?

He was the one man who'd ever told her he loved her. He'd proved years ago that those words had meant nothing to him. It certainly shouldn't matter now that he'd treated her with as little regard as he treated his endless parade of model girlfriends. So what if he'd bid on her just to show up his brother. His complete disrespect for her may make her want to run, but she wasn't tying double knots in her Nikes just yet.

By the time she removed the last batch of doughnuts onto the draining board and started on the glaze, her mind was set. Matt would get his date. She'd resent the hell out of him for it, but she'd go. The way she saw it, the resentment was just plain unavoidable. How dare he waltz back into her life after all this time and bid on her only to get back at Vic? How dare he hurt her like that merely as a side effect of showing up Vic?

Suddenly, she wished she'd added even more cayenne to the doughnut batter. Or maybe a dash of chipotle powder.

A glance through the diner's front windows told her dawn was just beginning to creep over the mountains. If anger wasn't still simmering in her veins, she might sneak out onto the street to watch the sunrise over the mountains.

Just then, a car drove past, its headlights reflecting briefly on another car, one she hadn't noticed before now, parked in the spot right in front of the diner.

"Huh," she mumbled aloud, cocking her head to the side, trying to get a better view of the car. It hadn't been there when she'd first arrived. Getting up at four to make doughnuts was the bane of her existence. As far as she was concerned, only an idiot would be out this early without reason. "So who would be out there now?"

The strange car made her more curious than nervous. She'd lived here most of her life and the crime rate in Palo Verde was virtually nonexistent, mostly just kids pulling pranks. There was no way that car belonged to a high school student. It was the kind of car that looked like it was going fast even when it was sitting still.

A glance at the clock told her there were still a good forty minutes before the diner opened. Too early for Jazz, her short order cook, to show up. Way too early for Molly or Olga, her two waitresses, to get here. Bless their college-student hearts, they always waltzed in at the last possible moment.

Besides, they always parked in back. And none of them drove glossy red sports cars. In fact, no one that she knew of in town drove a car that expensive. Or that ostentatious…

"Noooo."

She abandoned the whisk in the mixing bowl and headed for the front of the diner. Wiping her hands off on the towel she kept tucked in the strap of her apron, she shouldered her way through the swing door. By the bar, she paused, hands propped on her hips as she studied the car through the plate-glass windows. Her suspicions were right. The idiot was Matt Ballard.

Matt Ballard sat in his Lamborghini Murciélago Roadster staring through the window of Cutie Pies, watching Claire bake for far too long. He didn't even know why he'd stopped. Feeling too restless to sleep in the bed-and-breakfast where he'd booked a room, he decided to head out of town early. His drive down Main to the highway took him past Cutie Pies. He'd barely registered the well-lit interior of the diner when he found himself pulling into the spot right out front and cutting the engine.

That had been eighteen minutes ago at 5:03 a.m. At first, he'd assumed the lights were just security lighting. The kind of thing that stayed on all night long. But then he'd seen the flickering movement beyond the pass-through window and realized she was in there.

She'd be baking, of course. Cutie Pies was known for its doughnuts and pies. Someone had to get up frickin' early to make doughnuts for the morning crowd that would start showing up around six. He had trouble imagining Claire as that person.

That must be why he'd sat in his car so long. Because he was having trouble reconciling the idea that Claire was a businesswoman. Someone who got up before five.

The Claire he'd known in college had preferred to sleep until ten. She'd dreamed of designing clothes in New York. She'd loved British punk music and had five holes pierced in her ears. And now she owned a diner? It just didn't jive.

And like all puzzles it intrigued him. That was why he was here, sitting in his car, straining for a glimpse of her as she drifted gracefully past the opening of the pass-through window.

However, he certainly had enough sense to recognize that this was not healthy behavior. In fact, sitting outside anyone's place of business in the middle of the night could only be described as creepy. And a little pathetic.

Claire had always had this affect on him. For the few weeks they'd dated in college, she'd simultaneously brought out the worst and the best in him. Made him impulsive and illogical.

Last night's blunder was a perfect example. Why had he bid on her? How had he let the bidding get so out of hand? It certainly wasn't as though he wanted to go out on a date with her. Hell, he never wanted to see her again.

Which meant his best bet would be to put his car in Reverse, leave town before anyone was the wiser and simply let his date with Claire go unclaimed.

His hand was already on the ignition button when he saw her stop at the window and stare out. As if she was looking right at him.

She couldn't possibly see him, of course. Not in a lit room looking out into the dark. Still, he sensed she knew he was there. His instinct was confirmed when she disappeared for an instant only to reappear at the door in the dining room. She crossed to the door and stood there with her hands propped on her hips, glaring out at the spot his car occupied. When he saw her throwing the lock on the front door, he knew the gig was up and he climbed out of the car.

She was dressed in jeans and a pink T-shirt. Centered on the shirt was the image of a pie anthropomorphized with a wink and smile. The name, Cutie Pies, was scrawled over her right shoulder in a retro font. A white apron was tied around her waist, a towel tucked into it by her hip. Her hair was pulled off her face into a ponytail. Her face was clean of makeup. All in all, she looked far more appealing than any woman had a right to at five-thirty in the morning.

She'd never been conventionally beautiful. Her chin was a little too pointy, her nose a little too broad. Her mouth off balanced, with a perfectly sensible upper lip and a lush, sensual lower lip. Her face was more interesting than lovely. The kind of face you could spend hours looking at. The kind of eyes you could stare into endlessly, sharply intelligent, but still friendly.

Normally, that is. Today, her eyes were blazing with annoyance. "What are you doing here?"

She managed to make "you" sound like an insult. She stood in the doorway, blocking his way, leaving him standing out on the street. Her hands were still propped on her hips, her chest thrust out belligerently.

The sight of her made something tighten inexplicably in his chest. Indigestion, he hoped. Or maybe a heart attack. That would be better than the other possibility. That some long-buried affection was rearing its head.

He wished she looked worse, but what had he really expected? After all, he'd seen her on the stage just last night. But then, they'd been in a crowded room and separated by a distance of least thirty feet. Now she was mere feet away. And suddenly he was struck by the memory of what it had been like to kiss her. How hungry her mouth had always been beneath his. How her body hummed beneath his touch.

How many women had he dated since Claire? Hundreds, at least. So why was it he couldn't remember what a damn one of them smelled like, but he could still remember the scent of Claire's skin like she'd slept with her head on his pillow just last night?

He wanted to shake the memory from his body. To scrape it off his very soul. Every instinct he had roared at him to just turn and walk away.

As if sensing his indecision, she stepped back into the diner. "I've got doughnuts to ice. If you're leaving, just go. If you're coming in, lock the door behind you on your way in."

A wise man would have left. And he'd always considered himself on the smart side of brilliant. Still, he followed her into the dining room, sliding the bolt closed on the front door as she'd asked.

She looked up when he followed her through the swing door into the back kitchen.

"Hello, Claire."

"Whatever it is you want to say, you'll have to talk while I work." She stood with some kind of paintbrush in one hand and a frown on her pretty face. "The doughnuts have to be iced within a few minutes of coming out of the fryer or the icing won't set."

Her words caught him off guard. He'd expected a little groveling. Instead, her tone was brusque and impersonal. "Come on, don't be like that."

"Don't be like that?" she parroted back in apparent disbelief. "How am I supposed to be?"

"We didn't get a chance to talk last night."

"So you came by here now? You thought we could catch up for old time's sake? At five in the morning?"

Since that sounded both less creepy and less pathetic than, *I felt compelled to stop and watch you work,* he nodded. "Sure."

"Fine." But her acquiescence seemed forced, her tone pleasant, but overly so. She dipped the paintbrush into a bowl of milky white sauce and slapped some of it onto of the first row of doughnuts. "So how you been? Your millions treating you well?"

"What?"

"I guess that's rude to ask about your money." She dipped the brush again and moved on to the next row, leaving a messy trail of sugary goo in the wake of her brush. "Okay, how about this? So how's the weather out there in the Bay Area? I hear the summers are brutally cold."

"Stop it."

"Stop what?" Again she dipped and slopped.

"This. Talking about the weather. I didn't come here for small talk."

Instantly, the brush stopped, midswipe. Her head dropped forward and for a moment she was completely still. When she looked up, a mixture of chagrin and annoyance flickered across her face. Shaking her head she said, "Well, Matt, I don't think we're anywhere near ready for a big talk, so the small talk is all that's left."

"You're angry," he observed.

Studying her, he realized most people probably wouldn't realize she was angry right now. She kept it well hidden, but he knew her too well for her to hide it from him. How unsettling was that? He wasn't supposed to know her moods.

Claire just glared at him. "Ya think?"

"Maybe I'm missing something here." He shoved his hands deep in his pocket. "The way I see it, you don't have anything to be angry about."

"That's probably understandable. You've dated *a lot* of women over the years. You probably don't even remember me." Her voice was overly solicitous, like she was talking to an Alzheimer's patient or something. Only the slight emphasis on the words *a lot* hinted at her anger. "Let me jog your memory. I'm Claire." She pressed her hand to her chest. "You and I dated for six weeks in college. It was 1998. I know that's short even by your standards but—"

"Yeah, Claire, I remember," he interrupted, his harsh tone revealing far more of his emotions than he wanted.

"Oh, good. Because after last night when you didn't even seem to recognize that you were bidding on me, I wasn't sure."

Finally, her attitude pushed him over the edge. He reached out and grabbed her chin, forcing her to meet his gaze. "Stop acting like the victim here, Claire. You dumped me."

Her eyes blazed with anger as fierce as his own. "Yeah, I dumped you. But I—"

Abruptly, she broke off, her voice cracking as she dropped the brush and covered her face with her hands. He heard her breath catch and for a second he wondered if she was crying.

But then she lowered her hands and her eyes were dry, her expression almost rueful. "You're right. I'm not angry about what happened in college. I have no reason to be, right?" She gave a strangled sound that might have been laughter. "Is that what last night was about? Revenge for me dumping you?"

"Revenge? What's that supposed to mean?"

"You're the smart one. You figure it out." And just like that, she returned her attention to the doughnuts.

Was that really what she thought? He'd been so distraught over being dumped by her that all these years later he was still holding a grudge? Yeah, that was just what he wanted.

He moved around the worktable so he stood opposite her. When she said nothing, he reached a hand out and wrapped it around her wrist, halting her motions. "Bidding on your date wasn't revenge. I was doing you a favor." He smiled. To prove just how little she mattered to him.

But she wasn't looking at his smile. Her attention was glued to her wrist where his fingers rested against her skin. Suddenly, he was aware of her pulse thundering under his touch. Of the silken skin of the underside of her wrist. He sucked in a deep breath and got hit with the powerful blast of her scent. The aroma of freshly baked doughnuts and warm sugar mingled with the spice that was uniquely Claire.

The combination was as potent as a drug. Not that he'd ever done drugs. No, he had only two vices: pride and Claire. But he imagined this was just how a junkie felt. Twelve years, he'd been clean. One hundred percent Claire-free. He wasn't about to jump off the wagon now.

But damn he wanted another hit of her. Especially when she looked up at him with her green eyes wide and her chest rising and falling rapidly. He dropped her hand at the same instant she jerked it away from him.

"A favor is watching someone's dog when they're out of town." She rubbed her wrist against her shirt like she was scrubbing away his touch. "Or picking up some chicken soup at the grocery when they're sick. In what universe would bidding twenty thousand dollars for a date be a favor? What were you thinking?"

He propped his hands on his hips. His hand still burned from her touch, but he wasn't about to let her see that she'd rattled him. "What was I thinking? I was thinking the library could use the money and I could use the tax deduction. And, hell, I figured you would probably thank me. I remember that you haven't liked my brother ever since he cornered you during a football game your freshman year in high school and tried to cop a feel. I assumed you wouldn't want to go on a date with him and thought I'd help you out."

Her gaze narrowed as she wielded the brush like a sword. "Hey, I've been handling jerks like him since I turned thirteen and developed C-cups overnight. I could have handled your brother."

In that instant, he saw straight through her bristling anger to the fear beneath. He rocked back on his heels, unable to repress a cocky smile that he just knew would piss her off. "But what you can't handle is a single date with me?"

She blinked, brush hanging in midair. Her gaze met his, her eyes wide as she swallowed her surprise. Then she let loose a bark of laughter that sounded more nervous than amused. "Dating all those simpering models has clearly warped your brain. Obviously, they spend a little too much time stroking your ego while trying to get into your wallet. Don't forget, I knew you back before you were worth a gazillion dollars." She planted her hands on the counter and leaned in, issuing a challenge with her actions as well as her words. "So trust me. I can handle a date with you just fine. What I don't want to handle is the six months of gossip about you I'll have to listen to every day after you leave. I'm not worried about the date itself being anything more than an inconvenience."

He felt his smile slipping, but managed to keep it in place. Claire always had had a knack for twisting the knife. "The good news is, you can put your mind to rest. I don't plan on actually taking you on a date."

The brush slipped from her fingers to clatter to the counter. "Are you kidding me?"

"Don't worry. The library will get their money. I've already written the check. Obviously, neither of us wants to spend an evening in one another's company. There's no reason why we should."

"Oh, that is perfect." She scrubbed a hand through her hair. "After all these years, you show up in my life only to drag me into this pissing contest with your brother. You stir up all this gossip. And now you're trying to back out of the date? What is wrong with you?"

What was wrong with him? Christ, her logic was so twisted it made his head ache just trying to follow her train of thought. "You're the one who said you didn't want to go on a date with me."

"Yeah. I don't *want* to. But I sure as hell would go, if you would—" She broke off, frowning. "No. You know what? Forget it. You *are* going to take me on this date. You dragged me into the mess, the least you can do is have the decency to follow through with it."

"You said you didn't want any gossip."

"I don't want gossip. But I don't want pity, either. Thanks to last night, everyone in town thinks you bid on my date just because of the legendary Ballard sibling rivalry. If you don't bother to even take me out, it'll be worse than if no one had bid on me at all."

"Let me see if I've got this right," he said. "First you ream me for having the audacity to bid on you in the first place, then you give me hell for the kind of women I date, and now you're insisting I take you out despite that? Just how crazy have you gotten in the past twelve years?"

Her gaze narrowed slightly and he could all but see her figuring out which of his buttons to push. "Just crazy enough."

"Crazy enough to what?"

"To hunt you down and make you sorry if you don't hold up your end of this stupid bargain." Then she started ticking items off on her fingers. "I want it simple and to the point. Something low-key but highly visible. I want half the town to see us on our date. I want no romance and no drama."

He grinned wickedly. "Sounds like the perfect date."

Too bad he wasn't going to give it to her. He'd had enough of her calling the shots. He didn't know what kind of men she was used to dating here in Palo Verde, but he didn't take dictates from anyone.

Now that he had her list of do's and don'ts, he knew exactly how to piss her off. She was in for the most romantic night of her life.

Three

"I heard he chartered a jet and is going to whisk you off to some exotic, foreign locale," Olga said, her eyes lit with fervor.

Molly sighed. "So romantic!"

Claire barely suppressed her snort of derision. Molly and Olga, her two college-aged waitresses, were just so…young. So blissfully ignorant of the workings of the human male. Had she ever been this innocent? She didn't think so, not even when she was a teenager, constantly under the thumb of her grandparents, struggling with bitter resentment.

But of course, she had been this young. Briefly. When she'd been with Matt. It had been the one time in her life when she'd been filled with hope and optimism. A time when she'd believed she could have everything she'd yearned for but never thought she was worthy of. For that brief blip of time she'd imagined anything was possible. And it was the one time she'd felt as young as they seemed to her right now.

They stood huddled together, elbows propped on the counter, eyes gleaming as they talked.

"You know he's probably just bringing me to Palo Alto for dinner."

"Oh." Olga's gaze remained dreamy.

"Huh?" asked Molly. "Where?"

Olga answered before Claire had a chance. "Palo Alto. It's near San Francisco, where Stanford University is located. It's like the intellectual epicenter of California."

"I'm sure all the people at Berkeley disagree," Claire muttered, giving the counter a fierce swipe with her dishcloth.

Olga ignored her. "And it's where FMJ's headquarters are located."

Molly crossed her arms over her chest, clearly annoyed at being lectured to by Olga. "Sounds kind of boring."

"It's not," Olga assured her. "As far as Palos go, it's way better than Palo Verde."

Both the girls laughed, since everyone knew Palo Verde was just…unexciting. A smallish farming community halfway between Sacramento and Lake Tahoe, Palo Verde had little to distinguish itself other than the fact that it was the county seat and had some charming turn-of-the-century architecture. Molly and Olga were both attending the community college located on the outskirts of town. Though Palo Verde was slightly bigger than the nearby small towns they were from, it still offered few enticements for young women.

Which was probably why she didn't put an end to their musings. She knew better than anyone the frustrations of being young and trapped in a town smaller than your dreams.

So instead of reminding them that they were supposed to be rolling silverware, she took out a stack of bright pink cloth napkins and grabbed the tray of flatware herself.

"I bet he takes her to L.A. for dinner."

"Or Mexico!"

"Remember that episode of *Friends* when Pete took Monica to Italy for pizza? I bet he does that!"

"He can't do that," Molly said. "She'd need her passport, right?"

"Duh, she'd need her passport for Mexico, too," Olga pointed out.

They both looked at her. "Did he ask you to bring your passport?"

"No. He hasn't told me anything about the date."

In the week and a half since the bachelorette auction, she hadn't had any contact from Matt at all. Yesterday, she'd gotten a call from Wendy somebody at FMJ to inform her that a limo would be picking her up for her date at six that Saturday evening and that a hotel room had been booked for her, so she should pack an overnight bag. Claire wanted to tell Matt exactly what he could do with her overnight bag. However, the helpful Wendy had refused to connect the call. Claire had hung up, called information, gotten the number for FMJ and tried to get a hold of Matt that way. Only to be reconnected with Wendy.

Gritting her teeth at the memory, she focused on the task at hand. Lay out the napkin, add in the knife, fork and spoon, tuck in the points, roll. Sometimes getting lost in the minutia of life kept her going. Don't think about how your life didn't turn out the way you planned.

Don't think about the dreams you gave up on. Just focus on what's in front of you. Napkin, knife, fork, spoon, tuck, roll.

"So all you know is that he's flying you somewhere, overnight."

Both of the girls sighed again.

"So romantic!"

"It's not romantic!" Claire felt her general annoyance with the situation bubbling up. "Romance was Rick Blaine saying goodbye to Ilsa Lund on the tarmac outside of Casablanca with the Nazis bearing down on them. Him sending her away because it was the only way to keep their love alive. Romance was Harry running through New York City on New Year's Eve because he'd realized he loved Sally and wanted the rest of his life to begin that night. Romance is not a guy with way too much money, spending too much money, just to show that he has the money. That's not romance. That's ego."

Molly and Olga just looked at her like she'd sprouted antlers. Finally Olga cocked her head to the side and said, "He's trying to impress you. *That's* why it's romantic."

"He's not trying to impress me," she assured them. He knew she wanted a low-key date. Something that wouldn't attract a lot of attention. Instead, he was giving her this. He wasn't trying to impress her. He was trying to torment her. What a jerk.

Molly shook her head and said in a half whisper, "What does she know? How long has it been since she's even been on a date?"

"Too long," Olga agreed. "Since before I've known her, at least."

Claire ignored them. Napkin, knife, fork, spoon, tuck, roll.

Though it was a good point, not that she would admit it to them. After all, her one and only serious relationship had been with Matt and look how *that* had turned out. So what if she had zip practical experience with romance? She still had standards. She had the *idea* of romance.

"I can guarantee this." She flicked out another napkin. "Whatever this date is, he didn't plan it to be romantic." She dropped down a knife. "He's just showing off his wealth." She slammed down the fork. "Throwing around his money because he can. Matt Ballard is no different from any of the other Ballards in this town. They think they can get away with whatever they want, just because they're rich and influential." Drawing in a slow breath, she carefully centered the spoon, tucked in the corners with precision and rolled up the bundle. "There's nothing romantic about that."

Molly just shook her head. "Claire, you do not get out enough."

"Absolutely!" Olga agreed. "If some rich guy wants to spend a fortune on you, why not just enjoy it?"

Hmm…why not?

She set aside the last of the pink bundles and eyed the nearly empty silverware tray. One lonely fork remained. She pulled it out and ran her fingers along the rough spot on the handle as she eyed its bent tine. Like most things in the diner, this fork was worn and overused. It was always the last utensil left in the tray. Someone else might have just thrown it away, but not Claire. She held on to things. Still, it looked so sad, alone in the tray, she couldn't bear to put it back. Instead, she tucked it into the front pocket of her apron.

So why not just enjoy the date? Because Matt Ballard

was the devil himself. That's why. Because he was a lying scoundrel. Because he had no regard for all the things she cared about: hard work, doing the right thing, family. Holding on to the things that mattered.

Since this was obviously an argument she couldn't win, she poured herself a cup of coffee, adding a splash of cream and dash of sugar. Then she pulled the bent fork from her apron pocket and used it to stir her coffee. Sometimes, things served a purpose, even if it wasn't what they were intended for.

Satisfied, she sat on the corner stool and sipped her coffee, and she didn't look up again until the door swung open, the chime on the hinge signaling the end of their conversation as effectively as any argument she could have made.

Claire ordered Molly and Olga back to work as she delivered menus to the table herself, despite the fact that the Walsteads were regulars and knew every dish on the menu.

"Hey, Steve, Shelby." Claire greeted the two adults as she placed the silverware on the table. Then she ruffled the brown hair of the boy who sat beside his mother. "Hey, sport, how ya doing?"

He wiggled away from her touch with a playful grimace. "Fine."

"I know, I know," Claire groaned. "You're too old for that kind of thing."

Shelby smiled up at her. "I can't get used to it, either." Then she reached out and tickled her adopted son in the ribs.

"What can I get you to drink?" Claire asked, a warmth settling over her at the gentle interplay between Kyle and his parents.

Steve and Shelby ordered sodas and agreed when Kyle asked if he could order a shake.

She jotted down the order. "I'll get this right out."

Kyle's smiled beamed. Maybe as a way of apologizing for dodging her touch earlier.

Not that she minded. She remembered eleven all too well. That awkward stage where you desperately wanted to be an independent teenager and still longed for the comforts of childhood.

Watching Kyle with his parents, she felt a calm seep over her that she hadn't felt since Matt had returned to her life. No, she was not as young and hopeful as she had once been. But she was content with her life and the choices she'd made. Kyle had parents who loved him. He had happiness and security. She couldn't ask for more. She had sacrificed her relationship with Matt so that Kyle could have all of that.

The decision may have been hard at the time, but in retrospect, she was glad she'd done it. Since that fateful day she left Matt, she'd realized one important thing. The Matt Ballard she'd fallen in love with didn't really exist. He was nothing more than a figment of her imagination.

No, she could never love a man who willfully ignored a sweet and wonderful boy like Kyle just because it wasn't convenient to acknowledge him. But that was exactly what the real Matt Ballard did.

On the night of their date, she couldn't let herself forget that. No matter how much money he threw around, she'd never forget what a jerk he really was.

As Claire set the shake down in front of Kyle, she felt the slightest pang of regret, because he gazed up at her with eyes that looked so much like Matt's.

No, not regret. Sadness. Giving birth to him when

she was only sixteen had nearly ruined Courtney's life. When Claire had found out her younger sister was pregnant, she'd dropped out of college to help her. She'd left Matt to protect her sister and the child she'd carried. In the end her sacrifice had saved her sister's future, but not their relationship. Courtney hadn't contacted Claire in years. She'd never been able to make peace with the fact that Claire wanted a relationship with Kyle and his family. But the way Claire saw it, she was lucky the Walsteads were open to having Kyle's birth aunt in his life.

As strange as it seemed, Claire was far closer to the Walsteads than she was to her own sister. She supposed she could understand why Courtney didn't want anything to do with the Walsteads. Maybe for her, it was just too painful to see the child she'd never wanted and chosen not to keep. But more confusing for Claire was the way the Ballards treated Kyle and his parents. Vic looked enough like Kyle that anyone could see they were father and son. They all simply ignored it.

Of course, Claire had always known Vic was a jerk. Vic had been twenty when he'd gotten Courtney pregnant. His actions were reprehensible. Not to mention criminal—not that he'd ever been held accountable for them. Palo Alto was still a very small town and the Ballards were wealthy enough to keep the closet that held their skeletons firmly padlocked.

Still, Kyle was happy and that was what mattered. She couldn't have loved Kyle more if he had been her own child. But every once in a while, he did make her yearn for the children she would never have. And she sometimes wondered if they would have looked like Kyle, with Matt's eyes and her light brown hair.

She flashed a smile that she hoped hid her more melancholy emotions.

Kyle smiled back. "Thanks, Aunt Claire!"

By the time the night of their date rolled around, she still knew nothing. She had no idea what to expect on their date. Other than the plane, of course. But then again, everyone in town had known within about twenty minutes of Matt scheduling the flight at the nearby airstrip.

She'd once read in a magazine—years ago when she still followed news about Matt—that he owned a Cessna. So she'd expected him to fly her somewhere in that. But instead, the plane waiting for her on the tarmac was no mere single engine aircraft, but a veritable jet, sleek and long and reeking of wealth and privilege.

Of course, filthy rich, debonair Matt would own his own jet. She was still making payments on her decade-old car.

When she climbed out of the limo, Matt was standing there waiting for her, looking vaguely like James Bond, what with the tailored charcoal-gray suit, his perfectly styled hair, the snazzy sunglasses and the plane.

When he saw her, he slowly removed the sunglasses to study her. If he was disappointed in her appearance, it didn't show in his expression.

She owned exactly three dresses, all of which were nearly as old as her car. She'd borrowed this outfit—which consisted of wide-legged silk pants and a beaded vest with a matching shawl, all in a warm chocolate-brown—from Olga.

The limo driver took her bag out of the back and delivered it into the cabin of the plane. She'd debated for hours whether or not to actually bring a bag. She certainly didn't want Matt thinking she condoned being ordered around. Or worse that she was going to sleep with him. At the last minute, she'd dug an ancient duffel out of the back of her closet and thrown in a few things. She tried not to read too much into the fact that it was one of the bags she'd packed when she'd left him.

Now, the proprietary gleam in Matt's eyes as he looked at her made her feel vaguely queasy. She resisted the urge to rub her palms on her pants—after all they weren't hers.

"I didn't know what to wear," she explained, immediately regretting how insecure she sounded. The last thing she wanted was him imagining her stressing out over preparing for this date, though of course she had. "You didn't say what we were doing."

The left side of his mouth curved in a smile. "You look perfect."

Her chest tightened inexplicably. Dang it. He was not supposed to make her feel all fluttery. She gritted her teeth. And how dare he compliment her? Like he could charm her into submission.

"I assume," she said peevishly, "that's your plane we're taking."

He looked taken aback. "It is. How did you guess?"

She gestured to the scrawled name on the tail of the plane "*The Raven*? It's—" Then she snapped her mouth shut. "It was just a guess. Didn't you love that poem by Poe?"

But he'd caught her slip. He walked closer to her to stand less than a foot away. "The Raven was our project name for the nickel-metal hydride battery FMJ developed right after we went public."

Suddenly, she was aware of how tall he was. He'd

been an extremely late bloomer, still in the five-nine range when he'd graduated from high school, but he'd sprouted those last three or four inches in college. When she'd known him, he'd been just around six feet. Was it possible he was even taller now? Or maybe it was just that his shoulders were broader. Either way, he seemed larger than life. Certainly larger than her life.

And he was entirely too close. Close enough to read every emotion as it crossed her face. Nervously, she licked her lips and then wished she hadn't when his gaze traced the movement of her tongue as if she were a temptress.

"I must have read about it in the paper or something." The Raven battery project had put FMJ on the map. Matt had gotten nearly a dozen patents because of that project. It had made him millions, shot the price of FMJ stock through the ceiling and revolutionized the rechargeable battery market. All of which she'd known because she'd compulsively followed his career in the years following their breakup.

He grinned, sliding his hands into his pockets. "You had to read some pretty technical articles to know that."

She gritted her teeth. "Then maybe it was something someone mentioned in the diner."

"Which you remembered all these years? Ah, Claire, I didn't know you cared."

"I don't."

"Either way, you obviously haven't been able to leave your fascination with me alone."

"What can I say, people pick at scabs."

He threw back his head and laughed. Great, she'd meant to repel him with the analogy and instead she'd amused him.

"Are we going to go somewhere in this plane or did you just have me come out here to show it off?"

"We're flying to San Francisco. But not yet."

It was on the tip of her tongue to ask why he was taking her to San Francisco instead of Palo Alto. Yes, the two cities were just a short drive apart, but she'd just assumed he would take her to the city where he lived. But she certainly wasn't going to press the issue. Palo Alto was their old stomping grounds. It's where they'd dated and fallen in love. If he hadn't planned on rubbing her nose in the past, who was she to bring it up? Instead, she asked the other obvious question.

"Why not yet?" Just then, another car pulled onto the tarmac. She frowned, watching the green Toyota maneuver toward the plane. As soon as she recognized the driver, she whipped back around toward Matt and narrowed her gaze. "You have got to be kidding me."

He just smiled, walking toward the Toyota and holding open the door for the driver.

Out hopped Bella, the bubbly, overeager, annoying-as-hell reporter for the Palo Verde weekly paper.

"Thanks so much for calling me!" she effused, slinging the strap to her camera around her neck.

"No problem." Matt flashed Bella a charming smile.

Claire's stomach turned over in revulsion. How dare he try to manipulate this young woman? "Matt, you're wasting her time. Our date can't seriously be considered news."

"Oh, it certainly is!" Bella enthused. "Everyone in town is curious about why… I mean, everyone wants to know where he's going to bring you." The younger woman widened her smile. Gazing up at Matt like a groupie, she sighed. "I bet you have something really fancy planned."

Claire tried to resist rolling her eyes. Not that it would have mattered, since Matt was concentrating on charming Bella and Bella seemed determined to let him.

Sheesh, did young women these days have no self-respect?

And when had he turned into this smooth playboy?

The boy she'd known had been straightforward to the point of being blunt. He'd been all rough edges and geeky brilliance.

Of course, despite her earlier protests, she had followed all the gossip about him. She knew the kind of women he dated, so she'd guessed he'd changed, but reading about it in the papers and watching it from a front-row seat were two entirely different things.

"Why don't you two pose in front of the plane and I'll take a couple of shots?" Bella gestured them closer together, directing them toward the nose of the aircraft. Then she stepped back, eyed them through her camera and said, "Closer."

Matt stepped behind her, so his chest brushed against her shoulder. His hand settled between her shoulder blades and the musky scent of him muddled her senses.

"No, closer," Bella ordered cheerfully. "Put your arm around her."

Matt slung his arm over her shoulder, leaning close enough to whisper, "I swear I didn't tell her to do this."

"Oh, I believe you." She was beginning to realize the plucky young reporter was an instrument of the devil, gratingly cheerful and a total kiss-up. Evil geniuses weren't this diabolical.

"So tell me, Matt," Bella asked as she snapped some pictures. "Why did you bid so much money on Claire?"

"Maybe she's the love of my life." Matt made a show of nuzzling her hair.

The gesture sent warmth spiraling through Claire, which only annoyed her even more, especially in light of his sarcasm. She should not be attracted to him. She knew better. He was a first-class jerk and only an idiot would fall for his crap twice in her lifetime. She jabbed him in the belly, but he retaliated by grabbing her hand and bringing her knuckles to his lips.

She jerked her hand away. "He's joking. Aren't you, Matt?" She gave him a sharp nudge in the ribs. "We're just old friends."

"Really?" Bella looked up from her camera, her expression baffled. "I looked up your records at the high school. You were three years apart. I assumed you barely knew each other."

"We knew each other in college," Claire said through gritted teeth.

"Oh, I didn't realize you went to college, Claire," the evil Bella said with wide-eyed innocence.

"Just one semester."

Bella smiled brightly, meeting Matt's gaze over Claire's shoulder. "I graduated magna cum laude from the journalism school at UCLA."

Again, with the flirting.

Claire smiled sweetly at Bella. "In that case, the job market must be really tough for you to have ended up at a weekly here in Palo Verde."

Bella's smile turned down at the corners, but she

got the message. She wrapped up the interview quickly after that, but not before offering to send Matt a copy of the article if he'd give her his email address. When he told her to send it to his secretary, Bella's smile turned sour. She shot Claire a what-did-you-do-to-deserve-all-your-luck look then slunk away to her perky car. On the bright side, at least Wendy would have someone new to torture.

Claire didn't have long to enjoy her victory though, because a second later, Matt was guiding her into the jet. She'd never been in a private jet before and had no idea if the sleek leather upholstery and swiveling lounge chairs were standard-issue. Her fingers all but itched to caress the leather as she moved past the seat. Instead, she twisted the strap to her purse around her hands.

"I can practically hear Robin Leach."

"Who?" Matt asked.

"From *Lifestyles of the Rich and Famous?* Gram used to watch it obsessively. Every week." Matt just stared at her blankly. "Really? You've never seen it?"

He shook his head with an amused shrug. "Let me get you a drink and you can tell me all about it."

"Well, too late now," she muttered. "You're living it."

Before she could feel even more self-conscious, a smartly dressed woman in a navy suit and jaunty little cap stepped out of the cockpit and extended her hand.

"I'm Melissa. I'll be your pilot this evening."

"Oh." She glanced to the back of the plane to where Matt stood at a bar in the galley pouring drinks. "I assumed…" But she didn't finish the sentence.

She was so outclassed here, she should probably stop making assumptions of any kind.

"That Matt was going to fly you?" Melissa asked.

"He does have his pilot's license, so he usually flies himself, but he uses his smaller plane, *The Dove,* for those trips."

"Of course he does." Naturally this wouldn't be his *only* plane. Why not have two? Or a half dozen for that matter. "Technically," Melissa was saying, "*The Raven* is the company plane. Ford and Kitty fly back and forth to New York often enough to warrant it. Matt's never used it before for a date."

"Oh. I—" Claire broke off, unsure what to say. She'd assumed the private jet was just standard playboy fare for Matt. But apparently it wasn't. What was she supposed to do with that? Obviously, Melissa thought tonight really was some sort of hot date. Unsure what to say in response, Claire gave a weak smile and feigned interest in the trim work.

"Let me know if you need anything," Melissa was saying. Then, as if she sensed Claire's anxiety, she asked, "Is this your first time flying in a smaller plane?"

Claire nodded, glad to have an excuse to explain her nerves. "It is."

"You're in for a treat. It's not like commercial air travel."

Which Claire actually wouldn't know. She'd never flown before. Not that she was about to mention that to Mr. Owns-Two-Planes.

Melissa was right about one thing, Claire was definitely in for an unusual experience. But *treat* was not the word she would have used.

Four

Matt noticed Melissa giving him an odd look as she retreated to the cockpit. He'd never used *The Raven* on a date before. His Cessna was always his first choice, but for tonight he was pulling out all the stops. He was going to wow the socks off Claire.

At the front of the plane, the cabin held four chairs facing each other; the back held another pair of chairs as well as the sofa and the galley. He pushed aside the fantasy of Claire, vest unbuttoned, sprawled beneath him on the sofa. If her defensive posture was an indication, he wasn't going to get her anywhere near the back of the plane. At least not on the flight there.

For now, he'd have to content himself with getting her to unclench enough to set her purse down. Holding the bottle of wine in one hand and cradling the pair of champagne flutes in his other palm, he gestured to the seats. "Go ahead and have a seat. We'll be taking off soon."

She seemed to hesitate, as if gauging her chances at making a run for it. Her nerves amused him. She'd been so damn defensive the other morning at Cutie Pies. So angry, he could hardly get a word in edgewise, but now, he had the home-field advantage and he intended to use it.

She picked the corner chair, automatically swiveling to face off against him. A second later, the plane started inching forward and she braced her hands on the arms of the seat, her gaze darting nervously. He set the bottle in the bucket on the table and extended one of the flutes to her.

"Here. It'll calm your nerves."

"I'm not nervous!" she protested, but then the plane gave a slight bump as the wheels lifted off the ground and she ruined the effect by taking a gulp.

"I can get you something stronger. To calm your not-nerves."

Her gaze narrowed slightly so she was almost glaring at him, but at least she didn't look ready to faint. "No, thank you. After all, you've gone to all the trouble of getting champagne. I'd hate to ruin your complete lack of imagination."

"Actually, this is a Blanc de Noir from Napa."

She eyed the pale pink liquid suspiciously, as if he might have ruffied her. "Sounds fancy."

"I took a chance that your palate had developed beyond wine coolers."

Back when they'd dated in college, those had been her drink of choice, being both mild and cheap. Of course, at the time he'd drunk mostly lite beer for the same reason.

He lowered himself to the chair opposite hers. A plate of cheese and fruit was sitting out on the table and he nudged it toward her. "Try it with the grapes. They're from the same region and pair nicely with the wine."

Instead of following his suggestion, she leaned forward, the grapes untouched. "Tell me, Matt, what is it exactly you think you're doing here?"

"Excuse me?"

"The champagne. The fruit plate. The private jet, for goodness' sake. It's an awful lot of trouble to go through when you've already spent twenty thousand dollars."

"It really isn't," he said dismissively.

"No, it really is. I get it, Matt. You're worth *a lot* of money now. I knew that already. So why is it so important to you to rub my nose in it?"

"Is that what you think I'm doing?"

"It's obviously what you're doing. This isn't you." She gestured to the plane and the chilling bottle in the bucket. "You used to hate this kind of pretentious crap. And the way you acted with that reporter. She fawned all over you and you just ate it up."

Matt took another sip of the Blanc de Noir, relishing the cool slide down his throat. "You sound almost jealous."

Claire stilled, surprise registering on her face, as if that possibility had truly not occurred to her. She downed another gulp of wine. "Disgusted is more like it." Looking rattled by the idea, she shook her head. "I'm just trying to figure you out."

He set down his own glass. "Tell me something, Claire. What really bothers you about this situation? You claim to know how much I'm worth. You knew how much I spent to buy the date with you. This—" he mimicked her gesture toward the plane "—can't surprise you."

"You could have taken me to Luna across the street from Cutie Pies and I would have been pleased. More than. You would have spent a hundred dollars, tops."

"Would that really have satisfied your curiosity?"

"*My* curiosity? What's that supposed to mean?"

"You can't tell me you're not curious. About me. About my life. About what your life would have been like if we'd stayed together."

"You think I'm curious about *the money?* About some rich and fabulous lifestyle that you're living?" Her tone was sharp with disbelief. "Wow, you are really...well, *delusional* is the word that comes to mind."

"Fine," he said with a nod. "I'll let you pretend. I won't ask you how you knew about the Raven project or why you remembered that after all these years."

The look she gave him surprised him. It was so... patronizing almost. Like there was something big he'd missed entirely. Finally, she shrugged. "Okay, then. Let's say it was all about the money for me. What of it? Taking me on this date doesn't satisfy my curiosity. It only sows discontent. Makes me more miserable." Understanding lit her eyes. "Unless that's what you wanted. Unless this really was about revenge."

"Boy, you seem obsessed with this revenge idea."

She arched an eyebrow. "Just trying to figure all this out. All this money is a lot to spend on a date unless you're trying to make a point."

"Most women like having someone splurge big on them."

"Is that really your experience? That most women like this? This ostentatious posturing really works for you?"

Forget all her indignation. He'd seen her expression when she'd first stepped out of the limo. She'd been impressed. Just like every other woman he'd ever flown anywhere for a date. She just didn't want to admit it. And wasn't that interesting?

He smiled, not bothering to hide his satisfaction. "You'd be surprised how many women this works on."

She just shook her head ruefully. "I doubt it. Small-town cafés are just one step away from a therapist's chair. I know women pretty well. So, no, I'm surprised that this impresses some of them. For plenty of people, money is all that matters."

And then she pinned him with a steady, quiet look. For the first time since she'd walked back into his life, he felt all her anger slipping away, felt as though she was looking to the very core of him.

After a second, she looked away to gaze out the window, her expression unreadable. "What surprises me is that you put up with it. The Matt I knew had a very low tolerance for pretension. I can't imagine you wanting to be with someone who was here only for your money. I can't imagine you spending five minutes with someone like that. Forget the entire night."

He felt a pang of loss at her words. She was right, of course. In his friendships and his work life, he didn't tolerate people who were in it just for money. In FMJ's highly competitive research and development department—the branch he was in charge of—employees got by on their hard work and brilliance, otherwise they were shown the door. So why did he put up with that kind of thing in his personal life?

The only answer that came to mind was that he simply cared less about his personal life than he did about FMJ's success. He considered the idea for a minute. Wooing women with money was the path of least resistance. And since none of the women he dated were important to him, that was the path he took.

So what was he doing here with Claire? Did he really think the limo and the plane were going to impress her? Maybe. Yeah, maybe he had.

She was dead wrong about one thing: it wasn't revenge that motivated him. It was something more personal. She may claim to know how much he was worth, but knowing it and experiencing it were two different things. She may claim she didn't care about the money, but she was lying, if not to him, then to herself. Everybody cared about the money.

He wanted her to know exactly what she'd given up by leaving him. He wanted her intimately acquainted with what her life would have been like if they'd stayed together.

The limo and the jet were just the tip of the iceberg. The rest of the date was going to impress the hell out of her. And if he knew women half as well as he thought he did, she'd be begging him to take her back.

Claire wasn't sure what she expected for their date. Between her anxiety and her apprehension, she hadn't given herself much of a chance to consider the actual destination. Once the plane had landed in San Francisco and he'd moved her into the limo, she gave up badgering him for clues to where he was taking her.

What would he do next? Something ostentatious. Something guaranteed to highlight the difference between their social standings.

He'd said this date wasn't about revenge, and she'd realized on the plane that he was being honest. Or at least he thought he was. This wasn't revenge. He was merely putting her in her place.

Of course, she'd always known they didn't belong together. Even back in college when she'd thought he was her soul mate. Even then she'd known that he would always be richer, higher-class, better educated and smarter than she was. She'd just thought he didn't care about that sort of thing. Obviously, she'd been wrong.

He thought she was white trash, just like every other member of his family did. This was exactly like all the times when she was in high school when his brother, Vic, tried to cop a feel, but didn't really want to take her out on a date. Those Caldiera girls, they were perfect for fooling around with on the sly, but they weren't for serious relationships.

Tonight was that lesson on a grand scale. It was a point-by-point presentation of all the ways she just wasn't worthy.

She knew it for sure when the limo pulled up in front of a building with an elegant white marble facade. No grand sign or flashing lights identified the restaurant. Still she recognized the name etched in the glass of the double doors.

Climbing out of the limo, she blew out a rough breath and pressed her palm to her belly. "This is a Michelin three-star-rated restaurant."

Matt just smiled.

Located in the bustling heart of San Francisco's financial district, Market had earned a reputation for its simple but elegant atmosphere and its world-class menu featuring local and organic ingredients. Its chef and owner, Suzy Greene, had just launched her own show on the Food Network, *Greene on Green*.

Claire's feet felt heavy, but Matt's hand was steady at her back as he guided her through the double doors.

But she stopped stone still when they stepped inside. The restaurant was empty. At seven o'clock on a Saturday night. She turned to Matt in confusion. "How is this—"

But a woman's voice broke through her confusion. "Welcome to Market."

And there she was, Suzy Greene, walking across the empty space, arms wide and welcoming. She was shorter than she looked on TV, a petite little ball of energy with no-nonsense pixie-cut blond hair and a sassy smile.

She greeted Matt warmly with a kiss to his cheek before shaking Claire's hand. "Matt tells me you're a restaurateur, as well."

"As well?" Claire muttered. When confusion flickered across Suzy's expression, Claire felt obliged to explain. "I own a small-town diner. I wouldn't lump Cutie Pies in the same category as Market."

"Ah," Suzy nodded, smiling again. "But I'm sure the hassles are the same. Managing staff, keeping the customer base happy. The long hours. The relentless work." Then she leaned forward and whispered conspiratorially. "Balancing no time to exercise with an intense love of high-calorie food."

Claire had to laugh. "Yes, I do have that problem, as well."

Suzy linked her arm through Claire's and gave it a pat. "I can tell we're going to be friends."

Friends with Suzy freakin' Greene? She didn't think so. But the other woman was so nice, Claire could hardly protest as she was led to table set with large rectangular plates.

"That's why I knew I had to do something special for you when Matt told me about your date."

"Something special?" Claire looked again at the empty restaurant, her suspicion taking root.

"He's a very good friend," Suzy continued, ignoring Claire's question. "It's not everyone I'd let reserve the restaurant on such short notice."

"You shut down Market? For Matt?" Then she did a mental head slap. Obviously, the restaurant had been shut down. On a normal Saturday night, a place like this would be booked solid.

Then Claire started counting the days. It had only been two weeks since the benefit in Palo Verde. Even if he'd started planning their date the second he got back to town, that was less than fourteen days.

"That's crazy," Claire protested, shooting a look at Matt and then Suzy. "How on earth did you arrange this on such short notice? People must have had reservations for months now."

Suzy laughed. "They were very understanding when I explained. Besides, Matt offered to pay for their meals if they rescheduled. It's such a romantic story, how you two met again after all these years."

"Matt told you? About how we met again?"

"What a great story." Suzy sighed. Then immediately clapped her hands together. "I've had such fun planning the meal. I have a seven-course tasting menu that you're just going to love! I've paired each of the courses with a local wine. It's the most fun I've had all year. It's not often I get to play with no concern for budget at all." Suzy gave Claire's arm a squeeze and practically squealed with excitement.

"Oh, you shouldn't have," Claire said drily.

Suzy waved aside her protests. "I got to give most of

my staff the night off. They were thrilled." She gave a playful wink. "Don't worry, he's compensating me."

"No. Really. *He* shouldn't have."

A moment later, they were seated at the table with a plate of amuse-bouche between them. After explaining what each of the tempting nibbles was, Suzy excused herself to put the finishing touches on the next course.

As soon as they were alone in the dining room, Claire leaned forward and hissed, "I can't believe you lied to Suzy Greene to get her to clear out the restaurant for us. Suzy frickin' Greene! That's despicable."

Matt popped a micro-slice of cheese-topped asparagus into his mouth. "I didn't lie."

"Well, you clearly didn't tell her the truth or she wouldn't have been winking at me about how charming and romantic our reunion is."

He gave a c'est la vie shrug. "I may have left out a few details."

"Like what? Our mutual hatred and belligerence?"

He gave an exaggerated wince. "Now that's a little strong, don't you think?"

"No, I don't think—"

"Now that's the spirit. Don't think." He held an amuse-bouche toward her. "Here try this."

She wanted to protest, but when she opened her mouth he popped the bite in. The tiny dollop of goat cheese melted in her mouth, contrasting perfectly with the crisp fresh asparagus. Her eyes drifted closed as she savored the experience.

"See?" he said. "I knew you'd love it. Suzy's—"

His cell phone rang and he broke off with a frown. He pulled his iPhone out of his breast pocket and glanced at it. He frowned—for an instant his expression of intense concern flickered across his face, giving her a glimpse of the driven young man she'd known so many years ago. Then it vanished and he continued talking. "Suzy's one of the most talented chefs on this coast."

As he extolled the merits of Market—of which Claire was all too aware—he fiddled with his phone, turning it to vibrate. He slipped it back into his pocket. He was still talking a moment later when it gave a faint beep.

She raised her eyebrows. "Shouldn't you get that?" she asked as a waiter set a plate of appetizers in front of them.

"I don't take business calls on dates."

She was too hungry and too tempted by the food to ignore it, so she dug right in. In all likelihood, she'd never eat like this again; she might as well enjoy it.

"But this isn't really a date," she said. "And unless I'm mistaken, they called and sent you a text message in the past two minutes. It must be important."

"It's work," he said stiffly. "It'll wait."

When they'd dated in college, he'd been so passionate about the work FMJ did, work had never waited. He'd been on fire with the determination to solve new engineering problems. To invent. To create. To fix all the things wrong with the world, which he believed FMJ could do with the right funding and resources.

"What is it?" she surprised herself by asking. Not curiosity, she told herself. She was merely being polite. "This project you're working on? It's important enough that someone on your team is working on it on a Saturday night. So what is it?"

He sat back, his appetizer untouched, his arms crossed over his chest. "No woman wants to hear about some geeky science project over dinner."

The bite of Dungeness crab turned to sponge in her mouth. She set down her fork and sat back. Bringing her napkin to her face, she wiped at her lips. "I said that to you."

He lifted his glass of wine as if to toast her and then took several long swallows. When he set down his glass, he smiled with only a tinge of bitterness. "I should thank you. It's some of the best advice I ever got about women."

"Matt, I—" Christ, what had she done? He used to love talking about his work. "I'm sorry."

"Don't be. It was great advice." He shoved a bite of the appetizer into his mouth without even a glimmer of satisfaction.

"It wasn't advice. It was—" She broke off, dropping her hands into her lap.

When she'd left him, she'd been so worried he'd want to follow. She'd been so sure he wouldn't really let her go that she'd said things she knew would hurt him. That had seemed like the only way to make a clean break.

Now, hearing her words thrown back at her, she realized what she'd done. That womanizing playboy he'd become after she left—that guy she hated so much— she'd helped create him. She'd made Matt believe that she didn't want to be with the geeky brilliant scientist. And she'd been so convincing, he'd transformed himself into this suave playboy as a result.

"You were never boring," she tried to tell him.

"Tone down the geekiness and take out the wallet. Isn't that what you said? Well, you wouldn't believe how well that works with most women."

She couldn't stomach the bitterness in his voice or knowing that it had colored the way he saw women. The way he saw himself.

"Matt, when I left—" But she stumbled on the explanation. How could she make him understand the truth about the past? "Has it ever occurred to you that when I left, it wasn't about you at all?" His expression was impassive as he stared at some spot over her shoulder. She willed him to meet her gaze. To see the truth of her words. She searched her memory, dredging up all the awful lies she'd told him. "It had nothing to do with you being geeky or too smart or boring. It was none of that stuff."

"Then what was it about?" He spit the words out between them.

"It was about me and my family and—"

"Right. You're a family of runners. That's what you always said, right? So that's your excuse? You were just running away?"

She sucked in a deep breath, feeling like she'd been slapped in the face. Had she been?

She'd left Matt to return home and help her younger sister. Surely he knew that by now. Everyone in town knew why she'd come home and everything that happened since then, so surely he knew, as well. When she'd left Matt, she'd said so many things to make sure he wouldn't follow her, she barely remembered them all. Matt bored her. He was too geeky for her. She'd met someone else. She was going to New York with Mitch, a real man who rode a motorcycle and never talked about work at dinner.

They had all been lies. He hadn't bored her. She'd loved his passion for engineering. Most of all, there had been no Mitch. There'd been no one else. Ever. Mitch was a name she'd pulled from her mother's unsavory past.

But since he'd been back, it hadn't once come up in conversation. No "Hey, how's your sister?" or "So how'd that teenage pregnancy turn out?" He knew about it and clearly didn't want to talk about it.

But for the first time, she considered the possibility that she hadn't left only to help Courtney. Had she also been running?

The possibility made her skin prickle. Like she'd brushed against a live wire. Slowly, she shook her head. "I don't know. Maybe. I was so young. And scared. I loved you, but you—" She squeezed her eyes shut. "You loved me *so* much. Your future seemed so bright and I was terrified of ruining all of that."

She opened her eyes to see him staring at her, his expression dark and unreadable in the flickering candlelight.

And then his phone buzzed again, just the silent vibration of the phone moving in his pocket. He took it out and set it facedown on the table by his arm, but before he could say anything else, a waiter appeared, all solicitous concern.

"May I take this, sir?"

"Yes," Matt said. "We're done here."

The waiter left with their plates and still Matt said nothing about her confession. Obviously, he was going to ignore it. She didn't blame him and she hadn't really expected him to forgive her. Besides, he was good at ignoring things.

Finally, she leaned forward. "Look, this isn't working. This has been amazing, but it's enough, okay? The plane, the restaurant…by now, you've made your point."

"My point?" he asked slowly.

"Yes. Your point. I get it. You're very rich. You're also very smooth and very capable of wooing any woman on a date. But now, I'm just ready for it to be over because the stress—"

"No." He gave her an assessing look. "Why not just relax and try to enjoy the evening. Pretend it's just a normal Saturday."

"If this was a normal Saturday, I'd be at home watching *Dancing with the Stars* on my DVR."

His lips twisted in a wry smile. "Okay, pretend it's just a normal first date."

"I don't—"

"Right. You don't date. Well, pretend you do."

"Okay." She sucked in a bracing breath. "Normal first date."

With the man she both loved and hated. Easy as pie.

Five

The rest of the date passed in blur of food she barely tasted and wine she drank more of than she probably should have. At one point Suzy came out to the table to check on them and Matt invited her to sit with them for a while. Suzy seemed blissfully unaware of the tension between them. Matt seemed…thoughtful. As if he were assessing Claire like a specimen under the microscope and hadn't yet decided if she was going to become penicillin and save countless lives or merely make all the fruit on the counter go bad.

Claire felt her nerves drawing tighter and tighter.

His phone buzzed again and again. Each time he looked concerned, but he ignored it. However, it only ratcheted up her tension. By the time Suzy returned to the kitchen and the main course was whisked away, she'd had it.

"Stop acting like we're on a real date when we both know this is just a farce."

"A farce?"

"Yes. This is just part of the Twelfth Annual Ballard Festival of Putting Claire in Her Place."

"The Twelfth Annual…" He rocked back in his chair, turning his hands up in a what-the-hell gesture. "What's that supposed to mean?"

"Hey, you're the genius. You figure it out."

He dropped the legs of his chair forward and reached across the table to grab her hand. "Has my family been giving you a hard a time about this date?"

"No more than usual."

"No more than *usual?*" he repeated, his tone darkly steady. "What's that supposed to mean? Do they normally give you a hard time?"

The gleam in his eyes was almost…protective. Of her. Startled, she jerked her hand away. "Look, your family is…" She shrugged at the difficulty she had putting it into words. "They're your family. You know what they're like. Being a Ballard is everything. And they really get off on reminding people that they're the richest, most important people in town. Any chance they have to remind me that I'm just grasping white trash, they're going to take it."

His face slowly darkened as she spoke. "And you think that's what this date is about? That I'm putting you in your place?"

She couldn't read his expression and it unnerved her. She dropped her hand to the table and toyed with her fork. "Look, I…I don't know what to think this is about. You waltz back into my life after all of these years…" Her emotions choked her and she broke off, struggling for the words. "You take me on this amazing date. And

I'm so obviously out of my league here. I make grilled cheese sandwiches for a living and you introduce me to a woman who's won the James Beard award like we're supposed to be colleagues. And there's this elephant in the room between us that you seem determined to ignore. To ignore him and…"

Beside him his phone started buzzing again. It shattered her nerves. She slapped her hand down on the table, rattling the fork.

"Would you please just answer that!"

He stared at her, scrutinizing the lines of her face like she was a mystery he was trying to figure out. "No."

"Yes. Answer it." She looked away, unable to have this conversation with him now. Maybe ever. "It's obviously important. Your phone has rung six times in the past thirty minutes."

"I don't take calls from work when I'm on a date."

She threw up her hands in exasperation and then pressed both of her pointer fingers to her temples. "This isn't a date!" She blew out a long, exhausted sigh. Trying to let go of her anger. Trying to see him, not as the enemy, but as just a man, a guy on a first date with a woman. Like he asked. When she spoke again, she managed to make her tone civil. Logical. "Look, it's work. It's obviously important and you must know it or you could have just turned your phone off. I am a business owner, too. I understand. If someone from the diner were calling and needing to talk to me, I'd have to take the call. So, please, just answer it."

By now, the phone had stopped buzzing and lay silent by his hand. After a long assessing look, he nodded. Then he picked up the phone, bumped his chair back and stood. After punching a button or two on the phone, he turned his back on her, wandering to the far side of the empty restaurant.

"Ballard here."

Over the faint piped-in music, she could hear his end of the conversation.

"What?" His voice rose sharply. "How the hell did you do that? When I left you had two hours of work left. All you had to do was put the finishing touches on it, lock the door on your way out and leave it the hell alone until the shipping company came along to pick it up on Monday."

There was a faint babble as whoever was on the other end of the line rushed to explain whatever snafu had happened. Matt raised his other hand to pinch the bridge of his nose.

Then he cut off the other speaker. "You're fired. You're all—" He broke off, sending her a quick look. Like he didn't want to cuss in front of her. "You're all freakin' fired."

She heard another flurry of chatter from the other speaker.

Claire felt laughter bubbling up inside of her. His exasperation was palpable. She got up, crossed to where Matt stood and gently pried the phone from his fingers. She put her own ear to the phone and interrupted the speaker.

"Excuse me—"

"But the converter was working fine when—" a male voice continued.

"Excuse me," she repeated.

"Matt?"

"No. This is his date. Claire."

"Claire? Oh, damn! That's where he was? I am *so* fired. I—"

"You're not going to be fired. I promise." Matt tried to take the phone from her, but she swatted him away. "No, no. I promise."

"He's gonna kill me."

"He's not going to kill you." The voice on the phone was silent, but she could hear other voices in the background, a chorus predicting doom to them all. "Can I assume that whatever's wrong, you need Matt there to help you fix it?"

"I... Look, he's not going to leave his date. If I'd known he was out with you, I never would have—"

"Tell me your name."

"Dylan. Jeez, he is going to—"

"Just let me handle Matt. Don't worry. We'll be there soon."

She pulled the phone away from her ear. Matt tried to grab it back from her, but she dodged his grasp, and after finally spotting the end call button, hung up on Dylan's protests.

Matt stood watching her with a scowl on his face. She extended the phone back to him. "You should have let me fire him," he muttered as he took the phone.

She smiled sweetly. "Are you kidding? Dylan got me out of the most awkward date ever. He's my knight in shining armor."

"I'm definitely firing him."

She just laughed. "Come on, let's go. The limo can drop you at FMJ and then take me to the hotel."

Matt put a hand on her arm to stall her. "Wait here, I'll have Suzy box up dessert."

"But—"

"You can eat it at FMJ while I sort this out. I'm not carting you off to the hotel yet. As soon as I fix this mess, we'll finish the date. We still have a lot to talk about."

She suppressed a shiver as she watched him head for the kitchen. But the truth was, she'd love to visit FMJ, get a glimpse of the kind of projects they worked on. But underneath her excitement, she felt a tremor of dread. For the first time since Matt had waltzed back into her life two weeks ago, he seemed like the intense, passionate guy she remembered. And that made him very dangerous indeed.

Dylan turned out to be a scrawny twenty-two-year-old intern working at FMJ for the semester. He'd been given the job of getting a hold of Matt while the rest of the team worked on the problem. After the forty-five-minute drive from San Francisco to Palo Alto where FMJ's development lab was located, Claire was deposited into Dylan's care while Matt went to find out what was wrong.

"Take care of her," Matt had ordered. "Get her anything she wants." Then to her, he added, "Don't touch anything."

Claire had just laughed, but Dylan had nodded solemnly.

Matt left them standing near the elevator. The workspace was massive and open, with a scattering of scribbles on whiteboards set up amid the worktables and clusters of overworked lounge chairs. Bits of gadgetry were everywhere. It looked like the robotics lab of some deranged mad scientist.

The second Matt was out of earshot, Dylan started babbling again. "I'm so sorry I interrupted your date, if I'd—"

"It's no big deal," she tried to reassure him.

"Of course it's a big deal. You're Claire Caldiera. This was *the* big date, right? And—"

She shot Dylan a surprised look. "You know who I am?"

"Of course I do. You're—"

"I know. Claire Caldiera." She just wasn't used to people she didn't know talking about her without using the prefix *that trashy*. As in "That trashy Caldiera girl is up to something again." To Dylan she said, "I just assumed Matt never talked about me."

"Oh, *he* never talks about you." Dylan shook his head. "But the other guys do. The guys who've been around since the early days. Your name has…um, come up."

"I see."

Off in the far corner of the room, where Matt now stood, there was a team of six or seven guys and couple of women. A few of the faces were familiar. They were standing around an aluminum something. It was shaped like a giant dollop of whipped cream. The thing stood maybe five feet tall and was comprised of closely spaced arching blades that gleamed under the fluorescent lights.

"Is that a…?" she fished.

Dylan nodded like she'd guessed correctly. "Yeah. A magnetically-levitated, vertical-axis wind turbine. Cool, huh?"

"That's just what I was going to say."

One or two of the engineers standing around were people she recognized.

"Steve and Dean had just started at FMJ when Matt and I dated," she observed. They'd all been friends, back in the day. Now, when Steve glanced at her, his expression was suspicious. Dean gave a weak smile, but it didn't reach his eyes. "I can imagine the kinds of things they say about me."

Dylan's face flushed red and she knew she was right.

On the other side of the room, Matt looked up at her just then. He'd shucked his jacket and literally rolled up his shirtsleeves to get to work. His forearms were tan and muscled. Less than five minutes here and his hair, short as it was, was already mussed, like he'd been running his hands through it.

The sight of him, standing there with his hands on his hips, made her heart nearly stop. This was the guy she'd loved. The intense concentration. The sheer passion for his work. The brilliance.

In the times she'd seen him since he'd returned, he'd been all easy charm and smooth charisma. But now the Matt she'd loved so fiercely was standing right in front of her.

Oh, she was in so much trouble.

"Can I, um…get you a drink?" Dylan asked from beside her.

She smiled warmly at the poor guy. "Coffee would be great." She linked her arm through his and started guiding him toward an open door through which she could see a vending machine. "And you can tell me what it's like to work for Matt."

"It's great." Dylan sounded out of breath. Practically panting with enthusiasm. "I mean, he's Matt Ballard. He's practically a god."

"Um…sure." Here she was, ready to join the Matt Ballard fan club. Her and a twenty-two-year-old geek.

Four hours later, Matt found Claire, asleep, curled up in a chair. Someone had dimmed the lights in this half of the room, so she sat in the shadows, her legs tucked up onto the seat of the chair, her arms folded on the chair arm, her head resting on the bend in her elbow. Her hair had tumbled down around her shoulders; her makeup had lost its luster. Asleep, she looked so beautiful and relaxed, he didn't want to wake her.

In the time he'd worked with the rest of the team, he'd never once forgotten she was there. She'd spent the first couple of hours with Dylan. He'd gotten her coffee and they shared the dessert Matt should have eaten with her. She hadn't complained. Never distracted him or whined or demanded attention. Finally, she'd grabbed a book off the community bookshelf by the break room, curled up in the chair and read until she'd fallen asleep.

How many of the women he'd dated in the past decade would have handled this as well? He couldn't think of a single one.

He wanted to hate her. Wanted to resent the hell out of her, but, damn, she made it hard.

Maybe it would be easier if she wasn't so pretty. So vulnerable. Maybe if she didn't seem so convinced that he wasn't the only victim here. There were times when she seemed to think he was just as much to blame for their breakup as she was. Times when she seemed to be expecting him to apologize to her.

Who knew, maybe she was right. They'd been young and he'd been so devoted to FMJ. He'd probably been a crappy boyfriend. Tonight, she'd said it hadn't been about the person he was, but about her. Yes, she'd run, but the truth was, he hadn't gone after her.

Maybe all she'd wanted was for him to put her first. To make the sacrifice and chase her down. Things might have been very different.

After tonight, he knew one thing.

This thing between them wasn't over.

They'd only dated for six weeks. That was barely enough time to get to know each other then. The few times they'd seen each other since the charity auction wasn't enough time to get past her barriers, let alone to get reacquainted. And he was now willing to admit that that was what he wanted. He was ready to set aside all the things he thought he knew about her and to learn who she really was.

As gently as he could, he reached down, scooped her up into his arms and carried her out to the limo. She slept peacefully in his arms.

Claire woke up in the limo, with her head resting on Matt's shoulder and her shawl draped over her torso. His chest was beneath her cheek, the buttery fabric of his jacket soft beneath her skin, his heartbeat steady and strong beneath her palm. The woodsy smell of his cologne was faint and familiar and stirred something deep within her. The feel of his breath, warm against her hair, was the final proof that this was not just a dream.

She jerked upright, and felt his hand slip off her shoulder.

"You're awake," he said, rubbing his fingers over his own eyes, as if he, too, had been about to fall asleep.

Then his gaze fell on her. He seemed to be drinking in the sight of her. Warmth washed over her. Along with a solid dash of nerves. A glance at her watch told her it had been over seven hours since she'd gotten ready for this date. Her makeup was probably long gone, her hair most likely a mess. Despite that—and despite the fact that Matt had dated some of the most beautiful women in the world—when he looked at her like that, she felt beautiful. Like the overworked owner of a small-town diner must be exactly what he wanted most.

She tugged her shawl around her shoulders and shifted her feet to the floor, saying the first thing that popped into her head. "The book I was reading. I was going to borrow it. I don't suppose you—"

He shook his head. "I'll buy you your own copy."

"Oh. Thanks." She scooted across the seat, trying to put as much room between them as possible, but it was hard when her senses still felt muddled from sleep and her mind was still full of the dreams she'd had of him. Dreams of being held in his arms. Of having his hand stroke her skin. Of hearing his voice murmur soothing words.

To distract herself she asked, "The problem with the wind turbine. Did you get it fixed?"

"Yeah." He scrubbed a hand down his face, rubbing away the signs of exhaustion. "You have to know that if it hadn't been important—"

"Yeah. Dylan said there's some kind of big presentation in D.C.?"

According to Dylan, Matt had been working on it right up until he'd left to get ready for their date. They'd only had a few hours left of work to do when he'd left the rest of the team at FMJ. Which explained why he hadn't simply turned off his phone when he started getting calls. He must have known something had gone wrong. And yet he'd sat there, stubbornly refusing to interrupt their date.

Matt nodded. "Federal grant money, but the brass is expecting a working prototype in D.C. this week. And we had one this morning when I left work, but then some idiot spilled their drink on it and fried the motherboard.

Twenty million dollars of federal funding at stake and some idiot spills Red Bull."

She laughed. "I hope it wasn't Dylan. He seemed pretty sure he was going to get fired."

"Actually, replacing the motherboard should have been simple, but the mistake revealed a design flaw we hadn't seen before. That's the problem we were up all night solving."

"So the Red Bull was a good thing?"

"Sometimes the worst mistakes end up solving more problems than they create." Again he gave her one of those looks that could have melted the chocolate torte she'd had for dessert. He moved across the seat, closing the distance between them.

He reached out and brushed his fingers across her brow, nudging her hair out of the way. "Thanks for letting me handle it."

She swallowed. His touch was exactly how she'd dreamed it would be. His voice just as smooth and low. His breath just as warm.

"No problem," she murmured, her words coming out on a trembling gasp.

The heated glance he sent her stirred something deep inside, something that had been buried for years and that she thought was lost forever. Or maybe she'd hoped it had been lost forever. Either way, it was back. The faint churning in her stomach, the heat in her veins. The reckless need to shove aside thoughts of responsibility and the future. To simply seize what she wanted.

Because what she wanted was so close.

He leaned toward her, just as the limo navigated a sharp turn. The motion of the car rocked her off balance, and suddenly she was pressed against his chest, her palms flattened against his shirt. His heartbeat was strong and solid beneath her hand. His chest warm and muscled. He was no longer thin, as he'd been in his early twenties. Now he was all lean muscle. All strength and masculinity.

Her gaze fixed on the swath of skin at the vee in his shirt. The place where the long column of his neck met his collarbones, the hollow of his throat. Even though the interior of the limo was dimly lit, she could almost see his pulse. The steady rhythm of his heartbeat.

Then she looked up and met his eyes and felt the curious sensation of falling into her own past, into the memories she kept locked away, neatly pressed into the hope chest of her heart, where she never looked at them.

She'd worked so hard to forget the emotions he made her feel. The yearning. The hope. The love. She'd focused so much energy on that, she'd forgotten to bury the memories of their passion.

Now, she realized what a mistake that was. Because those memories came flooding back and she had no defense against them.

And then his mouth was on hers, devouring her. She craved his neediness. The full-throttle surge of his passion. Hot and dark. Tinged with all the buried emotions they'd kept hidden. It rose up inside of her, blocking out thought and logic. Blocking out all sense of reason.

When his mouth was on hers, all she could do was hold on tight as sensation poured through her. He tasted so familiar. Like all the hope and possibility of her youth. Like the freedom of finally being in charge of her own life. Like the infinite stretch of future happiness.

But it wasn't just the taste of him. The feel of his hair as it slipped through her fingertips. Of the hard corded muscles of his back as she nudged his jacket off his shoulders. Of his rough fingertips as he slipped a hand under the hem of her vest. His hands had always been large and now they felt massive, possessive, as he cupped her breasts, thumbing her nipples until her neck arched and she groaned low in her throat.

She knew then, this wouldn't be enough. A clumsy passionate kiss and a grope stolen in the back of the limo wouldn't satisfy her. She needed all of him. The passion pulsing through her was too great, and she trembled, already close to spinning out of control.

He was pressing into her, edging her back against the seat. In a second he'd be looming over her. In a minute—maybe five or ten—he'd have her half-naked. She'd tip over the edge. Lose control completely. Lose herself completely. Just like she had the last time.

She couldn't bear to give him everything of herself. But she couldn't bear to stop him, either. Tonight was a once-in-a-lifetime event. A moment out of time.

And it had been so long—so long—since she'd taken anyone to her bed. Longer than she wanted to think about.

She couldn't have him forever. Couldn't bear to let him go. It was twelve years ago all over again. Her life's misery in microcosm. So she did again what she had done then. She took control. Dealt with it on her own terms.

Planting both hands on his shoulders, she pushed hard, propelling him back. He broke away from her. His breath coming in rapid gusts, he fell back against the seat. Plowing a hand through his hair, he started to apologize. "I'm—"

But she didn't let him finish. She nodded toward the

glass barrier separating them from the driver. "That glass is mirrored or soundproof or whatever, right?"

Matt frowned, looking baffled. "Yeah."

She'd thought so. All evening long, she hadn't seen or heard so much as a peep from the driver. Before she could let herself think about what she was about to do, or what consequences it might have, or—even worse— what it might mean about her feelings for Matt, she kicked off her heels and shimmied out of her pants.

Matt didn't have time to do more than smile appreciatively as she climbed onto his lap, straddling the erection pressing hard against the zipper of his pants. His hands came to rest on her naked hips, just above the top of her panties. His fingertips were slightly rough against her skin. His thumbs traced circles around her hip bones, making her shiver with anticipation. She slowly lowered herself down, until the length of him pressed directly against her center. She rocked her hips back and forth, increasing the pressure. The sensation was exquisite.

Heat and moisture swirled through her as she brought her mouth back to his. He joined in enthusiastically, all apology lost. Which was exactly the way she wanted it. The way she wanted him.

Things would always be too complicated between them. Words only made it worse. This was the only way to communicate the want she felt. The need that consumed her.

And he understood perfectly. Touched her in exactly the right way. His mouth was just as hungry as hers. His hands just as desperate. His fingers shook as he unbuttoned the front of her vest and slipped it off her shoulders. He fumbled for a second with her bra and then it, too, fell away. His hands cupped her breasts, his thumbs scraping against her nipples. She pulled her mouth from his, arching her back, her breasts thrusting eagerly toward his mouth.

He smiled again, that slow lazy grin of his, one part charming rogue, one part naughty kid. Like a little boy about to dip his hand into the cookie jar who knew that what he wanted might not be good for him, but he wanted it too much to care.

He moved one hand to splay it against her back. Firm and possessive, he urged her closer to him. His mouth sought the tip of one breast. He laved her nipple with careful attention before moving to her other breast. His other hand slipped down to her thigh. His thumb nudged her panties out of the way and sought the very center of her. He found the moisture pooling there and then moved back to the sensitive nub between her legs. His touch was gentle but persistent, slowly stroking her in rhythm with his mouth on her breast. She was long past fighting the sensations he stirred. Every nerve ending in her body tightened as her climax rocked through her.

Her body had barely recovered when she reached for the top button of his pants. She didn't give herself a chance to second-guess herself. She couldn't think. Didn't dare to. Any regrets she would have, she would save for tomorrow. She allowed herself only enough foresight to be relieved when he produced a condom from his wallet. She couldn't get it onto him fast enough. Her breath caught as she sank down onto him. The pressure of him inside of her—the feel of him deep in her core—was exquisite. But it was the expression on his face that made her chest tighten.

She could almost believe that she was everything he ever wanted. That she was his deepest fantasy come to life.

She wanted him to look at her like that forever. She couldn't bear knowing she'd never see that expression again. She squeezed her eyes shut, blocking out the pure yearning that she didn't want to feel, choking back the tears she didn't want to cry. Unable to bear the feeling, she channeled all her emotions into this moment. She rode him harder, blocking out everything but the feel of him buried deep inside her.

As he climaxed, he ground out her name with such emotion that she almost wished she'd done things differently. She almost imagined the life they could have had. If only there weren't so many secrets between them. And so many things that had gone unsaid.

Six

Claire didn't know what to eat for breakfast. Most mornings, the answer was easy. Roll out of bed and mindlessly make her way to Cutie Pies to make other people their breakfast. She worked seven days a week. And though she didn't always work eight-hour days, she was always there for breakfast, Cutie Pies's busiest time. Over the course of the morning, she always ate something. At a restaurant, finding food was easy, even though she rarely prepared a meal for herself.

Now, for the first time in twelve years, she didn't have to be at the restaurant first thing in the morning. In fact, she wasn't even in Palo Verde.

Her internal alarm clock hadn't allowed her to sleep past five. Her internal emotional alarm hadn't allowed her to fall back asleep after waking in Matt's bed. In his arms.

Last night, she'd been so sure that by *deciding* to have

sex with him, she'd be taking control of the situation. As if the logical act of choosing could eliminate the emotions of her heart. As if it could protect her.

In the dim light of morning, she recognized that reasoning for the lame excuse it was. Lying in Matt's bed, his naked body pressed against her back, his arm resting heavily across her ribs, his hand cupping her breast, she'd felt a welling of contentment so strong it made the backs of her eyes burn.

In that moment, she'd faced the truth. Sleeping with him had gained her nothing. *Choosing* to do so had been an illusion.

She was as vulnerable to him as ever.

A single night of passion made no difference one way or the other. This would end. He would inevitably remember that she was a Caldiera and he was a Ballard. That their families were eternally at odds. That she was just grasping white trash to his wealth and privilege. And when he did he would walk away from her and return to his real life. She'd be crushed when he did. Her only hope now was to try to maintain some shred of dignity.

So she'd slipped out from under his arm, scrounged for some clothes and snuck downstairs to forage for breakfast. She'd pulled on the jeans and shirt she'd packed in her overnight bag, but the morning was colder than she was used to, so she grabbed a Stanford sweatshirt she'd found draped over the back of a chair.

Arms wrapped around her waist she considered the contents of his refrigerator. Five bottles of Sierra Nevada Pale Ale, half a stick of butter, an empty jar of dill relish and a half gallon of milk, which—she popped the cap and sniffed—had gone bad.

She scanned the countertops. Matt lived in a 1940s

foursquare located about two miles from FMJ's head-quarters. Last night, the limo driver had taken them most of the way back to San Francisco to the hotel where Matt had booked her a room. But after they had made love, she didn't want to experience the sterility of a hotel room. She wanted to see his home.

From the outside, the house had a quaint charm that blended perfectly with the other homes in the neighborhood. On the inside, it had been renovated to a pristine modern sleekness. All the surfaces were either a creamy white or a warm cocoa-brown. The gourmet kitchen was done in the same style with sleek modern cabinetry, brown/black granite and gleaming industrial-quality appliances. She'd bet her thirty-year-old griddle his Aga range had never been used.

However, some helpful decorator had furnished his kitchen with large glass canisters filled with flour, sugar and coffee. A survey of the pantry yielded a few more staples. With the meager supplies and her mind still spinning, she did what she did best when facing a problem. She baked.

Matt woke to the highly unusual sensation of being perfectly content. And to the smell of something baking, which was even more unusual, since as far as he knew, the only time his kitchen had been used was three years ago when Ford had recruited him to host the FMJ holiday party and the caterers had used the ovens.

He pulled on jeans, but went bare-chested because his favorite Stanford sweatshirt had gone missing. As he made his way downstairs, the unmistakable smell of coffee and fresh-baked biscuits grew stronger. He paused at the arched doorway to the kitchen, propped his shoulder against the jamb and watched Claire puttering around by the sink as she washed dishes. She hummed as she worked. Don McLean's "American Pie," unless he was mistaken.

For a minute, he just stood there, content to watch the mesmerizing sway of her hips as she scrubbed and rinsed. The waistband of the red sweatshirt hit her right at hip level. How could a woman so completely covered still look so damn good?

Then she paused, tilted her head slightly and sniffed the air. No timer had gone off, but she seemed to sense the biscuits were done and went to the oven. She wrapped a towel around her hand and pulled out a pan he hadn't even known he owned.

When she turned to place the pan on the island opposite the oven, she saw him. She stilled instantly, her eyes wary.

Scratching his chest, he commented, "I would have sworn I didn't have enough food to satisfy a cockroach. How did you manage to make biscuits?"

"I'm good at making something out of nothing," she said as she busied herself removing the biscuits into a towel-lined bowl she'd set on the counter.

He poured himself a mug of coffee and gulped down a hot mouthful, ignoring whatever implication might have been hanging in the air between them. Claire was good at a lot of things. In particular, she was good at overthinking.

He wasn't about to let her do that now. The fact that she'd been up long enough to bake biscuits from scratch in his bare-bones kitchen meant she had a head start on him.

So he rounded the island, took both her hands in his to stop her from fussing with the dish towel and turned her to face him. He cut off any protest she might have made by kissing her soundly until he felt her melt, all liquid warmth and homey goodness, against him.

He backed her up, step by step, until her hips bumped against his, trapping her between him and the counter. Pulling back, he kept one hand planted on her hip so she was firmly anchored to him. Then he reached into the bowl and withdrew one of the biscuits. The flaky crust yielded to the pressure of his teeth. His eyes drifted closed. A little salty, with the hint of butter, so light it nearly dissolved on his tongue. Perfect. Almost as perfect as she was.

"I suddenly understand why men used to keep women chained in the kitchen."

She gave a shove to his shoulder. "Sexist pig!" But her tone was playful. That wariness was gone.

He chuckled, not releasing his hold on her hip. "You may be right, but that doesn't mean it's not a turn-on that you're as good in the kitchen as you are in bed." It was a heady combination, having the woman he'd just slept with make him breakfast. As he chewed, another wave of bliss swept over him. "Most of the women I've dated wouldn't lift a baking pan unless it was filled with diamonds."

She pulled back from him slightly, a frown marring her face. "Then you and Suzy…" The question hung between them for a second before she finally wiggled free and held up her hands. "Never mind. I don't want to know."

Turning her back on him, she headed back for the sink, but he snagged her arm and reeled her back in. Her mouth formed an O in surprise and he popped a bit of biscuit in.

"No. Suzy and I never…" He paused, mimicking her

unasked question. "Never dated. Never anything." He added just to be clear. "She's just a friend."

"Oh."

"Is that so hard to believe?"

"It's…" She seemed to mulling over her word choice. "Unexpected."

That he could believe. "What would you like to do today? I did happen to date the assistant director of the Monterey Aquarium. I can give her a call and—"

"I have to go back Palo Verde today." She pulled away from him again and this time he let her go. She grabbed a biscuit and retreated to the stretch of counter near the sink. "I was planning to leave just after breakfast."

He glanced at the clock on the oven. "It's barely seven. And it's Sunday. Take the day off."

She just shook her head. "I own a restaurant. There are no days off. Olga agreed to open for me this morning, but they'll need me there soon. Before lunch if I can make it."

Her determination was written clearly on her face, from the set of her jaw to the tension around her mouth. This wasn't a battle he'd win.

He tossed the last bite of biscuit in his mouth and dusted his hands off on his jeans. "Okay. I'll call Melissa and have her get the plane ready. We can be at the airstrip in an hour. Which will put us back in Palo Verde well before noon."

"Us?"

He didn't like that edge of suspicion in her voice, so he spoke firmly. "Yes. Us."

She gave her head a little shake as she set her biscuit aside, largely uneaten. "You don't need to fly back with me."

"Yes, I do. Think of it as walking you to the door."

"That's not—"

"What's this really about?" Was she somehow embarrassed by what had happened between them? She hadn't seemed to feel that way last night, but who knew what was going on in her mind now.

For a long moment she was silent. She broke off a bite of biscuit, but instead of eating it, she squashed it between her fingers. "Last night was great. But I think we'll both be better off if we acknowledge it for what it was."

"And what was it?" That was the crux of the matter, wasn't it? Women and that pesky urge they had to define relationships.

As far as he was concerned, last night had been great. And he wasn't willing to give her up just yet.

She continued rolling the bit of biscuit between her fingers like a worry bead. "To be honest, I don't know what last night was. An aberration. A mistake, maybe." Her lips curved into a slight smile, but it was one she didn't share with him. "It was damn fun, that's for sure. But I don't think I can put a label on it."

"And that scares you," he concluded.

Her gaze darted to his in surprise. "No. That's not the problem."

"Then what is?"

"This thing between us. It doesn't have a future. Whatever it is, it's over."

At the words *it's over*, Matt swallowed hard, choking down the last bit of suddenly dry biscuit.

Last night the passion between them had sparked hot enough to singe hair. The memory of her touch was seared into his skin. He'd never felt so out of control or so close to heaven with any other woman. So this thing between them, it wasn't even close to over.

She didn't believe it, either. He could see that in the set of her jaw, like it was all she could do to force the words out.

"Fine," he said simply.

"You agree?"

"This isn't over, but if you need to tell yourself that it is, I'll let you do that."

She frowned. "You haven't always been this autocratic."

"You must be remembering wrong."

"I'm not." She pushed away from the counter. "Surely you can see that this relationship has no future. There's no point in continuing on if—"

He closed the distance between them in a few quick steps. One additional step had her hips trapped against the countertop and her body pressed to his. He lowered his mouth to hers. She tasted of tangy biscuits and smoky coffee. He shouldn't have wanted her again already, not after the night they'd had. Yet he did. The mere sight of her in his sweatshirt had made him hard and the taste of her on his lips made him strain against his jeans.

He felt her resistance melt under his touch. Felt her protests die before they even formed in her mind. Her hands fluttered to his shoulders and her fingers pressed needfully into his skin. Her hips bumped against his. He could have her again. Here in the kitchen, up against the counter. He could strip her naked and make love to her right now.

As much as he wanted to do just that, he forced himself to pull back. When her eyes fluttered open, he met her gaze steadily.

"*This* is reason enough to continue."

With deliberate care, she extracted herself from his

embrace. "It's just too complicated. We'd never make it work. There are too many obstacles between us."

"Right now, the only obstacle I see between us is my old Stanford sweatshirt and I can have that off of you in about three seconds."

"Don't be obtuse," she chided, as if unsure whether to be annoyed with him or charmed by his tactics to get her into bed.

"I'm not being obtuse," he said slowly. "I just don't see any reason not to take you back to bed and keep you there."

"Okay, we live in different towns for starters."

"Kitty and Ford have houses in Palo Alto and New York City. They make it work. We're a twenty-five-minute flight away from each other. That's barely a commute."

"Okay, then there's your family."

He set his jaw at a stubborn angle. "What about them?"

"They hate me and think I'm trash. For starters."

"Well, I'm not so fond of them, either."

"Then *my* family."

"What?" He held up his palms in a gesture of confusion. "Now your sister doesn't like me?"

"Don't be an idiot." She retreated around the island in the center of the kitchen. "That's not what I mean."

"Look, I'm not the one being an idiot." He planted his hands on the counter and leaned toward her. There it was again. This implication that there was some big obstacle between them that they couldn't work around. "There may be things between us, but you're making them all sound worse than they are. Whatever it is, we'll figure it out. Unless you're dying of cancer and haven't told me,

I don't think there's anything we can't eventually work out. I think this is just you trying to run away again."

"What if I am?" She asked the question, half belligerently, half defensively.

He studied her for a moment before a slow smile crept across his face. "Then I'm going to have to chase you."

Claire just looked at Matt, wanting to roll her eyes at his arrogance. "I don't think you were half this annoying when we dated in college."

"Of course not. I was too in love with you."

"Were you?" she demanded. He'd backed her into a corner and she resented it. "*Were* you in love with me?"

He slanted her a surprised look. "You doubt that?"

Suddenly, the entire tone of their conversation changed. The very air around them seemed to vibrate with all the things between them that had gone unsaid, the way the atmosphere is charged just before a thunderstorm.

"Yes. I…" The words caught in her throat as she searched his face, taking in the strong line of his jaw, the faint jut of his chin that gave away he was clenching his teeth. That said so much about what he didn't want to reveal. As did the fact that he hadn't answered her question outright. The things he wouldn't tell her told more about how he'd felt than any words he'd spoken.

But wasn't that true of her, as well?

That first morning, she'd said they weren't ready for a big talk. Maybe they never would be. It's not like she wanted him to know she'd never really gotten over him. Yet, surely he'd guessed that. They'd slept together for goodness' sake. She could hardly pretend to be unaffected by him now.

She forced herself to meet his gaze. "You seem surprised that I could doubt you."

The only indication that he'd heard her was a slight narrowing of his gaze. "I had told you I loved you."

His tone was carefully blank. Devoid of emotion. As if he was speaking of another person entirely. Another lifetime.

A memory flashed through her mind of the first time he'd told her he loved her. The image of his face above hers as they made love, telling her over and over again, "I love you. I'll always love you."

She'd had to squeeze her eyes closed against the rush of emotion. The absolute truth in his gaze had seared itself in her mind. She'd never forget it. And she'd tried. God knows she'd tried to scrub it from her mind.

"Yes," she said now. "You did say the words. So many times. And I believed you. I never doubted it. I wished I could have."

"Because it would have made it easier to walk away from me?"

"Yes," she admitted baldly. And she could tell that surprised him. "You didn't expect me to admit that, did you? If I'd thought you didn't really love me, it *would* have been easier to leave you. It also would have been less heartbreaking to watch you move on."

Part of her wanted to study his face, to watch him for any flicker of emotion at what she was revealing. But she found she couldn't make herself look at him. She felt far too vulnerable, her heart laid bare for him to judge or scorn.

So she continued without giving him a chance to respond. "You'd sworn you loved me. That you would never stop loving me, no matter what. But then, we hadn't been apart more than—what was it, a couple of weeks?—before you started dating someone else."

"Marianna," he said softly.

"Marena," she corrected him. "God, how pathetic is that? I remember her better than you do." She tried to laugh, but it sounded brittle.

"How did you even know about her?"

"My friend Rachel told me. Saw you at a party, actually, and snapped pictures of you together. She was the first person I knew to buy a digital camera and she took pictures of everything."

"How very helpful of her," he said wryly.

"She was trying to be helpful. She didn't realize we'd broken up. I'd only been gone a week or so. She didn't even know I'd dropped out of school."

"Claire—"

"Maybe I shouldn't have minded. After all, I introduced you to Marena." A week before she'd broken up with him, he'd driven across town to pick her up from a study group. He'd arrived so early, he'd sat at a nearby table and waited. Afterward, she'd introduced him to the other girls from her economics class. "But when Rachel emailed me those pictures—" To her embarrassment, her voice cracked and she had to swallow back her tears.

More images she'd never been able to erase from her memory. Marena dressed in a microskirt, her body pressed against Matt's, his hand cupped possessively on her backside. Claire's stomach had churned at the sight and she'd barely made it to the bathroom before losing her lunch. Her sister had come in just after, nauseated herself, and they'd sat on the bathroom floor together and cried. Funny, but that was the moment her sister,

Courtney, really started trusting her. After that, she knew there was no going back. They were in it together.

"Of course, that was just the beginning." Claire continued. "Six months later, FMJ went public. You guys were millionaires overnight. And you were, what—just twenty-one, twenty-two?"

He didn't give a precise number. Was he reliving the glory of those first weeks? Or trying to decipher her own emotions?

"You were celebrities. It seemed like every move you made was in the paper."

"You must have been looking pretty hard to find news about FMJ in New York."

She shot him a glance, frowning. Was he baiting her or did he really not know?

"I was back in town by then. Working at Cutie Pies. I couldn't turn around without someone telling me about you. About the parties you'd thrown, the hotels you'd trashed. The supermodels you'd dated and dumped."

"We didn't trash any hotels. That was a rumor. We just happened to be staying at the same hotel as Courtney Love."

"Exactly. You lived like a rock star."

"And it never occurred to you to wonder why I acted that way?" There was a note of anger in his voice. As if this was her fault.

Her gaze snapped to his face. "Of course I wondered. That's the point, isn't it?" She'd been at home, cleaning up the mess his brother made, while Matt had been moving on with his life. Partying like a rock star with every scrawny model he could lure into his bed.

Of course, she hadn't known at first that Vic was the one who'd gotten Courtney pregnant. Courtney had refused to tell anyone who the father was. When she' finally relented and told Claire it was Vic, Claire had been incensed. He was four years older than Courtney. He'd committed statutory rape. But at sixteen—and even eighteen—Courtney had refused to admit that he had manipulated her into his bed. She'd refused to go to the police and had told Claire she'd deny it if Claire went on her behalf. In a small town like Palo Verde, Claire knew she'd have a hard time getting the police to act even if Courtney had been eager to point a finger.

Then Claire had resented Matt all the more. He'd already broken her heart by moving on so quickly. The speed and fervor with which he'd recovered from his broken heart seemed proof that he'd never loved her at all. Against the backdrop of her life in Palo Verde, it was all too easy to believe the worst of him.

That old bitterness leached into her voice as she hurled the words at him like an accusation. "You were supposed to love me. I was supposed to be the love of your life. 'I'll always love you.' Isn't that what you said?"

"And you think the way I acted meant I didn't love you? It never occurred to you that I dated all those women because I couldn't have you?"

"What occurred to me was that *always* meant something different to me than it did to you."

"What are you saying, Claire?" he pressed, his voice thick with anger. "Do you expect me to believe you still love me? Because if *always* meant anything to either one of us, we'd still be together."

The emotion in his voice surprised even Matt. He rarely lost his temper, and he hated that Claire brought him to that. Over and over again it seemed.

Even worse, he hated the stung expression on her

face. As if he'd slapped her. Or snatched a piece of candy away from a child. And worse, even still, was the way his breath caught in his chest while he waited for her to respond. "You left me for another guy. You rode off to New York on the back of Mitch's motorcycle and never looked back. So don't tell me how hurt you were when you saw pictures of me with Marianna."

"Marena," she said blankly.

"What?"

She met his gaze, her eyes wide, but steady. "Her name was Marena."

Funny he couldn't remember her name. Hell, he barely remembered her. But Mitch was a name seared into his memory. He'd never even met the guy, but his hatred for him still sat heavy on his chest like a cancerous tumor. He'd once refused to hire an innocent intern just because his name was Mitch.

After all this time, he was still waiting to hear whatever sorry excuse she could cough up about Mitch. He deserved an answer.

Before he got one, the doorbell rang.

He turned to look at the front door, just visible through the doorway that lead from the kitchen to the dining room and the foyer beyond. Then he glanced at his watch. "It's barely seven. Who the hell rings the doorbell before seven on a Sunday morning?"

In the moment he was busy looking at his watch, she slipped right past him.

"That's the cab I called after I put the biscuits in the oven."

Only then did he notice the overnight bag that sat at the foot of the stairs. She snatched it into her hands on her way past. Before he could stop her, she was halfway out the front door.

She paused just long enough to look over her shoulder at him. "Don't worry about flying me back to Palo Verde. I can get home on my own."

And then she was gone.

Only after she left did he notice the bite of biscuit she'd been toying with as she'd talked. She'd flattened it onto the counter, like a squashed bug. A casualty of her stewing emotions.

Maybe she thought she was hiding her resentment because she hadn't been facing him when she spoke. He may not have seen the betrayal on her face, but he certainly heard it in her voice.

He crossed to the spot, pried it up with his thumb and dusted it into the sink. Ever since that morning at the diner, he'd wondered why she was so mad at him. She'd dumped him. What right did she have to be angry?

Well, now he had at least part of the answer. She was mad about how quickly he'd moved on after she dumped him. But he still didn't understand why.

Their breakup had been brutal. In addition to extolling the virtues of Mitch and his motorcycle, Claire had listed his myriad flaws. He was too boring. Too smart. Too busy working to have fun. He wasn't what she wanted and she was tired of pretending otherwise.

But if any of that was true, why had she cared what he'd done afterward or who he'd dated? And why had she followed FMJ so obsessively in the news? And she must have followed it obsessively to know about the Raven.

But why? And why lie about it now?

Clearly, Claire thought their discussion this morning heralded the end of their relationship. He'd seen it in her eyes when she looked at him that last time. She'd been saying goodbye. But this time, he wasn't letting her go.

Besides, she'd stolen his favorite sweatshirt.

Seven

"Where did he take you on your date?"

She'd heard the question from friends and customers alike. From blue-haired, eighty-year-old women and giggly teenaged girls.

The one person she didn't expect to hear it from was Kyle, who sat at the counter eating the grilled cheese sandwich she made him every Wednesday after school. Wednesday was the one day during the week that both his parents worked late and he'd taken to hanging out at the diner. Steve and Shelby were gracious enough to act like she was doing them a favor by letting him sit there and do his homework, when in fact it was always the highlight of her week.

However, she had not expected Kyle to ask about her date with Matt. Certainly not after his years of feigning complete disinterest in all of the Ballards.

Like everyone in town—everyone with eyes,

anyway—Kyle had figured out his relationship to the Ballards. Since Kyle had his grandmother's distinctive almond-shaped, whisky-colored eyes, as well as her strawberry allergy, it was pretty obvious which family genes had contributed Kyle's Y-chromosome. Kyle had figured out the truth when he was seven.

He'd come to Claire to ask about it. "I wouldn't want Mom and Dad to think they're not enough," he'd explained. At the time, she'd told him the truth as simply and as honestly as she could. Of course, he'd known she was his aunt by blood for as long as he'd known he was adopted. The few times he'd asked her about his birth mother, she'd been able to honestly say that she admired the decision Courtney had made to give him up for adoption. At sixteen, Courtney was smart enough to know she wasn't ready to be a mother. Giving Kyle up was the greatest gift she could have given him and moving on with her life away from Palo Verde was the best decision she'd made for herself. But Claire had a much harder time explaining about Vic.

At seven, Kyle hadn't yet been old enough to understand how distasteful—not to mention illegal—it was that Vic had gotten such a young girl pregnant. And he certainly didn't understand that Vic's crimes had gone unacknowledged by most of the town merely because Vic was from a wealthy and powerful family. All Kyle knew was that his birth father lived right there in town and never so much as smiled at him.

Even at seven, he'd been astute enough to know that if the Ballards hadn't acknowledged him yet, they were unlikely to do so at all.

And that had been the last time Kyle had mentioned the Ballards to her. Until the Wednesday after her date with Matt, when he sat there, poking listlessly at his sandwich.

She was so surprised by Kyle's question, she just sat there for a long moment, staring at him, dishcloth hovering over the counter she'd been wiping down. Finally, she tucked the cloth into the tie of her apron. "Just a restaurant in San Francisco."

Kyle stabbed a slice of fried zucchini. "What's he like?"

"Brilliant," she answered without thinking. "Stubborn. He doesn't tolerate fools or people who don't work hard. And he never—" She broke off abruptly, suddenly aware that she was not only serving her own selfish need to talk about Matt, but feeding Kyle's curiosity about him, as well.

Kyle sat very still on his stool, his expression carefully blank. She knew instantly that his facade of disinterest hid a spark of curiosity. A glimmer of hope. Kyle was as sensitive as he was smart. She alone knew how hurt he was by the Ballards' cold rejection. She hated to think that he might be harboring any anticipation that Matt would feel differently.

Kyle had been hurt so many times by the Ballards, she couldn't stand to see him hurt again. She leveled her gaze at him and said, "He's a good man, but he's still a Ballard."

"I know." He nodded seriously, before shoveling several more zucchini fries into his mouth. "You're not going to marry him, are you, Aunt Claire?"

"Nope. Not a chance." She didn't bother wondering who had put the idea in his head. Seemed like the whole town was obsessed with the idea that Matt was going to…she didn't know what people expected to happen. For him to fall in love with her? Come back to town and sweep her off her feet? Ride through town on a white horse to rescue her from a flame-spouting dragon?

Well, actual dragons flying through town were more likely.

Kyle, excruciatingly polite kid that he was, waited until he'd swallowed before saying, "That's good. Even Mom thought that was why he'd come back. But I told her you'd never leave Cutie Pies."

Claire felt her head sway, as if the world had suddenly come to a stop under her feet. "What do you mean, 'He'd come back'?"

Kyle may have been smart and polite, but he lacked the social experience to recognize the shock on her face. So he didn't know to soften the blow, but came right out and said, "You know, come back to stay in town. He's Mom's new client. He's why she's working late tonight."

Kyle's mom worked as a real estate agent. And if she was working late this evening because of Matt, that meant he was already in town.

Sheesh, no wonder people thought they were dating.

And then, suddenly her heart started pounding a rapid tattoo inside her chest as the bigger realization hit her. If Matt was working with Kyle's mom, how long would it be before Matt ran into Kyle? Hadn't the poor kid been through enough without the additional humiliation of meeting Matt only to be rejected by him in person?

Before she could even consider the implications, she looked out the plate-glass windows overlooking the street to see Shelby and Matt climbing out of his Batmobile, which he'd parked in the space directly in front of the diner.

She felt a burst of pure protectiveness. It was one

thing for Matt to toy with her emotions. She wasn't about to let him meet Kyle. The poor boy had been hurt enough by the Ballards. She couldn't let Matt do any more damage.

Matt hadn't believed he could sneak back into town unnoticed, but he hadn't been prepared for quite as much attention as he attracted. He'd checked in to a B and B on Comal Road late the night before. Despite the hour, the woman who owned the place seemed all too eager to socialize. Since he'd been up early and put in a full day at FMJ before making the drive in the afternoon, he hadn't been in the mood. Still, the woman mentioned at least twice that she knew Claire through the local chamber of commerce and that she and Claire were "practically friends." He'd considered sneaking out early and heading to the diner for breakfast, but the B and B's owner had been so determinedly chipper about serving him breakfast that he'd had little choice but to choke down the short stack of pancakes and scrambled eggs.

And that was just the start of it. People seemed far more talkative than they had just a few short weeks ago when he'd seen many of them at the library fundraiser. Everywhere he went, people wanted to stop and chat with him. Mostly about Claire.

The general consensus was that, besides serving the best doughnuts in the state, she was an angel from heaven. The verdict on him was still out.

It made for an oddly unproductive day. He'd hired a real estate agent, Shelby Walstead, to serve as his excuse for returning to town. After all, FMJ had been looking to open an additional R & D lab and Palo Verde seemed as good a place as any. Though Ford and Jonathon were in D.C. for the week, he'd cleared the idea with them via a conference chat. Ford thought the idea was brilliant. Jonathon hadn't said much but hadn't shot down the idea, either. The tax incentives would be in their favor, the local economy could use the boost and—most important of all—it would keep Claire in his sights for as long as he wanted her there.

However, the real estate agent he'd hired only made it through three of the properties she'd planned on showing him, none of which were remotely suited to FMJ's needs. The woman had to be the least successful Realtor in the history of the profession. She was as nervous and jumpy as if he were her very first client. Finally, he'd decided to put her out of her misery and suggested they stop by Cutie Pies for a break.

She must have known what a crappy job she was doing and feared he was going to fire her, because she paled, then finally nodded before mentioning that her son sometimes hung out at Cutie Pies after school and she'd be glad to have the chance to see him.

He slid his car into the spot in front of the diner, unsure of what his reception would be. He hadn't had a chance to talk to Claire since she'd run out the morning after their date. She'd been dodging his calls. He'd gone to the trouble to hunt down her email address, but she'd ignored his emails, too.

So he was surprised by how she marched out of the diner to meet him in the street. Until he saw the anger glittering in her eyes. Her hair was pulled back into an efficient ponytail; her face was bare of makeup, her cheeks flushed. She looked refreshingly simple and appealing dressed in jeans and a Cutie Pies T-shirt. It didn't bode well for either of them that he found her indignation charming.

She faltered when she saw the real estate agent, obviously struggling to muster a smile.

"Hey, Shelby," Claire was saying, as she ran her hand over her hair, smoothing down hair that wasn't out of place to begin with. "You here to pick Kyle up or just to check in on him? 'Cause he's doing great. Just sitting there at the counter like he always does."

Shelby returned an equally strained smile. "Well, I did think…"

Inside the diner, Matt could see a boy sitting on a stool near the wall, a ball cap obscuring his features, an oversized backpack on the counter beside him. One that looked like it would dwarf his small frame. Matt had a flashback to his own youth, when he'd hung out at Cutie Pies after school because it had been easier than dealing with the dysfunctional dynamic at home.

The boy on the stool turned to look out the window, straining his neck to see the adults chatting on the street. He sat with his elbows propped behind him on the counter. For a moment, there was something so familiar about the situation, Matt had the odd sensation he was looking at some past version of himself transplanted into Claire's diner.

Claire interrupted Shelby, who'd been rambling about something or other.

"Why don't you go on in, Shelby? I wanted to talk to Matt for a few minutes anyway."

"Oh!" Shelby looked pointedly between them, her gaze wary. "Sure. Matt, why don't we start again in the morning? That way you and Claire can catch up."

"Great idea!" Claire responded for him. Before he could protest, she linked an arm through his and steered him away from Cutie Pies. She shot one last look through the front window and then zoomed Matt down the street.

Main Street ran straight through the center of town, dead-ending at the county courthouse on one end. The park was just a short distance away. She seemed to be steering him in that direction.

Despite her claim to want to talk to Matt a few minutes alone, she didn't say anything so he asked, "You know Shelby well?"

"What?" She looked at him, startled. "Shelby? Yes. I mean, as well as could be expected, I guess."

"But well enough for her to trust you to watch her kid sometimes," he pointed out, wondering about her evasiveness. Claire was blunt and to the point. Always. So what was up now to make her hem and haw?

"Oh. That. Well, we're practically family." She scrubbed her hand across her forehead. They'd reached the edge of the park now and she turned off onto the walking trail that winded across the green. Her voice was suddenly fierce. Almost protective. "Kyle's a really good kid. He's smart. The kind of kid that figures things out and—"

He stopped, pulling her to a halt beside him. "Claire, what's up?"

"What's…up?" She sounded more angry than confused.

"Yes." He searched her face, taking in her wide eyes and flushed cheeks. "You're rambling. Get to the point."

She sucked in a deep breath, then bit down on her lip. Then sucked in another breath, preparing to launch some kind of verbal offensive. Finally, she spoke in a rush. "You can't move here."

"What?"

She started walking again, her words pouring out of her at an equally fast clip. "You hated it here. I can't imagine why you'd want to look at houses. You can't seriously be thinking of moving back. It wouldn't be fair to any of us. Not even you."

"I'm not."

Spinning to face him, her gaze searched his face, no doubt looking for signs of subterfuge. "You're not?"

"I'm not looking at houses. I'm looking at real estate for FMJ. We're looking to expand our R & D lab. Ford thinks Palo Verde may be the perfect location. Particularly if we can find an existing building that only needs minor renovations."

"So *you* wouldn't be moving here."

"No. Our headquarters would still be in Palo Alto."

He stepped closer to her, trying to read her expression in the dabbled light of the shady park. As soon as he'd said he wouldn't be moving there, relief had flickered across her face. But something else, as well. Something he couldn't read.

As for the relief, well, that wasn't exactly a balm to his ego.

"Look," he finally said. "I know why you're so upset."

"You do?" Her voice sounded high and squeaky again.

He hated that she seemed so nervous. So unlike the Claire he knew. He fought the urge to pull her close to him. In the quiet sanctuary of the park, they were alone without being really alone. Chances were, no one was watching them, but he wasn't going to risk it. So he shoved his hands deep into his pants and rocked back on his heels.

"Yeah. All that gossip you tried to warn me about, I got a taste of it today."

"Oh." She pressed her hand to her belly. Then seemed to realize for the first time that she still wore her little apron. She reached behind her to tug the tie loose and pulled the apron off.

"Everywhere I went today, people asked me about you. The general consensus seems to be that I must have fallen in love with you during our date."

A burst of laughter broke through her clenched lips. She didn't respond, but focused her attention on rolling the apron into a tight little tube.

Unable to resist any longer, he nudged her chin up with his knuckle. "You aren't under that impression though."

"No." She shook her head. Her tone sounded… sad maybe, but not disappointed. "I know that's not a possibility. And it's not what I want, either."

"Good." As hard as she was to read today, he could see the truth in her answer. "That's a relief. Because the people of this town seem very protective of you."

She quirked an eyebrow, some of her tension melting away. "They do?"

"Yes. I had several people warn me to treat you right. And one old lady with hair the color of beets told me that if I broke your heart she'd hire one of those guys from *The Sopranos* to break my kneecaps."

Finally, Claire laughed, a genuine bark of laughter that seeped into his soul. "That would be Mrs. Parsons. She eats at Cutie Pies every Monday for lunch and watches way too much TV."

"Obviously."

"But she's harmless. And on a fixed income, so I doubt she could afford to hire Paulie Walnuts."

"Good to know. Because that Mrs. Parsons had me worried."

She shot him a look of pure exasperation. "You know, I'm trying really hard to be angry with you right now. And I don't appreciate you making it so difficult."

Her annoyance was palpable. In fact, she looked pretty darn close to stamping her feet and shaking her fist at him.

"I didn't come back here to make things more difficult for you."

"But you did." She sighed. "Make them more difficult, I mean."

"I'm going to be here another week or two, more if I find a property."

She looked up and her gaze met his. "You can be away from FMJ that long?"

"The B and B has wireless. I'll work remotely. Drive back for the day if someone spills any more Red Bull on a two-million-dollar piece of equipment."

"Well, that's a relief."

Was that actual relief buried under her sarcasm? Once again, he gave in to the urge to touch her. Just reached out his hand and trailed a finger down her cheek. She shivered in response. Her sensible mind may tell him she wanted him to leave, but her body said something else entirely. She still desired him. Just as much as he wanted her. It was that logic of hers he'd have to get past.

"I can't promise I'm not going to pursue you while I'm here. This thing between us isn't over yet, Claire. We both know that."

She stepped away from his touch. "I told you I don't want—"

"You told me you don't want complications in your life. That's not the same thing as not wanting me."

"Maybe. But I can't have one without the other."

"And if you could?"

"I can't. It's a moot point. At the very least, there's going to be gossip and speculation. And when you leave, that's just going to make things that much harder on everyone."

"That's what you're worried about? Gossip?"

She shot him another one of those you're-an-idiot stares of hers. "That's *one* of the things." She ran her apron through her fingers, twisting the cloth into tight figure eights.

"What if everyone just thinks we're friends?"

"Friends? That ridiculous."

"Is it?" he asked. "People are only going to gossip about us if they think there's something interesting going on. There's nothing less exciting than two people not having sex."

"So you think if we pretend to be just friends that people will lose interest?"

"Exactly."

"That's the stupidest thing I've ever heard."

He had to laugh at the sheer indignation in her voice. As if his unworthy idea was an affront to her intelligence. He might be more annoyed if he didn't suspect that her attempts to pick a fight weren't just a way for her to alleviate the sexual tension between them.

She just glared at him, his laughter only making her fume more. "You're supposed to be a genius," she accused.

"I am a genius." Which he knew was not the same thing as being smart about people. He never had excelled in that arena, something his brother had never let him forget growing up.

"Then try to be a little smarter." She blew out her breath in a huff. "No one is going to believe we're just friends. If we're spending time together, people are going to assume there's something going on. They're going to gossip."

He took a step closer, but she backed away. "Are you saying you're so attracted to me that you can't be around me without people knowing how you feel? That your feelings are too strong to hide?"

"Of course not," she scoffed, backing another step away, practically inviting him to follow.

"Because as hard as it's going to be, I can hide my feelings. Can you?"

Her spine straightened indignation. "Of course!"

"Good." He took another step closer until she bumped against the tree at her back. He propped his arm on the trunk beside her head, leaning in toward her. "Because the way I see it, either we pretend to be friends in public, or I pursue you in public and leave no doubt about what's going on between us."

"And if I agree to go along with this silly plan of yours? If we pretend to be just friends in public—" she looked up at him, her gaze wide, her breathing shallow "—then do you promise to stay away from me the rest of the time?"

He smiled, relishing her obvious discomfort. "Hell, no."

Claire didn't trust Matt. Especially since he'd sworn mere seconds ago to keep his hands off her in public, yet now he had her wedged between his body and a tree. He hadn't touched her, but he stood close enough that she could feel the heat radiating off his body. She'd dashed out of Cutie Pies without grabbing her jacket. The crisp fall air only urged her to lean into him, to absorb all that heat for herself.

He didn't close the distance between them, as if he were waiting for her to make the first move. The worst part of it was, she wanted to. Arch her back, tilt her neck, raise up onto her toes and she'd be pressed against him, her lips just under his in an unmistakable invitation.

One he wouldn't refuse.

But a temptation she couldn't give in to.

She planted her palm on his chest, relishing the firm strength of his chest muscles. She arched onto her toes, but angled her head so her lips hovered beside his ear. She drew in a deep breath full of his scent and then whispered, "Back off."

Giving his chest a firm shove, she got him to move only because she'd surprised him. He laughed as he stumbled out of the way and she dodged under his arm.

Holding her palms out as if to ward him off, she pronounced, "I'll go along with your plan only because I don't have any choice. I can't stop you from looking at properties here, but let me go on the record as saying that I think this is a very bad idea. And I don't trust you for a minute."

He feigned shock. "Don't trust me? What's not to trust?"

"I don't trust your motives. And I certainly don't trust that you're a man of your word."

His lips curved in a slow, smug smile. "Considering the only promise I've made is to do everything in my power to lure you back into my bed, I guarantee you can take my word for it."

"That is *not* what I meant." She bit out her response word by word. Sheesh. There were times when she just wanted to wrap her hands around his throat and strangle him. Which was so much better than the times she wanted to wrap her hands around other parts of him. "I don't have a choice in this, do I?"

He grinned. "Not at all."

"I'm not sleeping with you again, so you can get that idea out of your head right now."

"Yes, ma'am." His gaze ran down her body and back up, leaving no doubt exactly which thoughts were taking up permanent residence in his brain.

She nearly growled in frustration. She *so* didn't need him egging her on.

As annoyed with herself as she was with him, she stalked toward the exit of the park, desperate to stay one step ahead of him. With any luck, Kyle and his mother would be gone from Cutie Pies by the time she and Matt made it back.

She'd seen Kyle's interest in Matt and it worried her. If they met, one of two things would happen. Either Matt would ignore the fact that Kyle was his nephew, which would hurt the boy's feelings. Even worse was the possibility that Matt would acknowledge Kyle. It was all too easy to imagine Matt temporarily befriending Kyle only to hurt him more when Matt left Palo Verde for good.

With any luck, the week Matt was planning on being here would pass quickly without Matt and Kyle ever coming face-to-face. And then, maybe, it wouldn't hurt Kyle so much when Matt left. As for herself, well, by now she was pretty much doomed to get hurt no matter what. She sure didn't trust luck to protect her.

Claire had never had much faith in luck. It tended to

turn around and bite her on the ass. And that was the real reason she was going along with Matt's plan.

The only way to guarantee that Matt didn't have a chance to hurt Kyle was to make sure they didn't meet. The only way she could guarantee that was to spend as much time with him as she possibly could. If she kept him distracted enough, he'd coast through the week and be gone before she knew it.

His plan to avert gossip wouldn't work, of course. But then, she didn't think that he thought it ever would. Matt was used to getting what he wanted. In this case, he obviously wanted to spend the week chasing her. Well, he was going to get what he wanted. She'd let him chase her, but he wasn't going to catch her.

Eight

Matt could take apart and put back together any gadget he got his hands on. He could decipher the technical specifications for any product his team developed. He'd authored or coauthored over fifty patent applications. He'd led his R & D team at FMJ to create so many groundbreaking products that one of the local magazines had recently named him "The Man Most Likely to Save the World."

But when it came to women…well, they were still something of a mystery. Sure he knew how to please one. That was a simple matter of biology. Understanding what went on in their minds was another matter entirely.

The mysteries of one female brain were all he could handle at a time. Which was why he decided to ignore the fact that Shelby Walstead obviously didn't like him. Which at least partly explained why he was so easily distracted in the following week. Shelby was supposed to be showing him properties. But any time he had even the barest excuse to play hooky, he took it.

"What do you mean you've only seen five properties?" Jonathon asked via videoconference four days later.

Matt was sitting on the back patio of the B and B where he was staying. He had his email open at the bottom of the screen and a pair of windows open at the top for the three-way videoconference. Ford's image was visible in one window, Jonathon's in the other. Even when they were all traveling, they chatted at least weekly, though they worked best when they were all together. Though Ford was the CEO of FMJ, Jonathon had always had the strongest "vision." He was the unspoken bully of the playground, keeping them on task, when they were likely to be distracted.

"Give him a break," Ford jumped to Matt's defense. "He's only been there four days. And no one likes to look at real estate."

Since he couldn't let Ford do all the defending, he said, "I don't think she likes me."

Jonathon rolled his eyes. "What are you, ten? Stop worrying about Claire and—"

"Not Claire. The real estate agent. Where'd we find her anyway?"

"Wendy hired her. And it doesn't matter if she likes you. Just go see the properties she shows you and make a judgment call so you can get back here."

"At least tell us things are going better with Claire," Kitty chimed in from over Ford's shoulder.

"No," Jonathon grumbled. "I don't give a damn how things are going with Claire. He should focus on looking at properties."

"Things are great with Claire." Matt forced some enthusiasm into his voice.

Great. That was strictly true. He was certainly spending enough time with her. Each morning he went to see one property with Shelby, during which time the woman was professional, but uncommunicative. After that, he stopped by Cutie Pies for lunch. He'd spend the afternoons with Claire.

She'd turned into some sort of maniac cruise director. Apparently, she had taken his challenge to feign friendship for the sake of the town quite literally. Each afternoon she'd scheduled some "friendly" activity for them to do together. They'd entered a chess tournament at the senior center. They'd joined a tour bus on a trip to the local apple orchards. One afternoon she'd even dragged him to the elementary school to judge the science fair. The activities were so wholesome, even he was starting to believe they'd never slept together.

"There's no point in staying there if you're not accomplishing anything," Jonathon pointed out.

"Progress may be slow," Matt said defensively, "but if there really is a viable property nearby that's perfect, trust me, I'll find it."

"Find it fast. Your team is getting antsy without you. Neither Ford nor I speak geek quite the way you do. Without you here to translate, productivity has come to a screeching halt. I stopped by the lab yesterday to check on things and I interrupted a Final Fantasy tournament."

Matt chuckled. "That sounds like them." His team of engineers were brilliant, but sometimes…high-strung. Coaxing work out of them could be taxing. But when you presented them with the right challenge, they could work miracles.

"You don't have to sound so proud," Jonathon

groused. "We never have this kind of problem when you're here."

"You make it sound like I never leave the office."

Ford chuckled. "You never do leave the office. When was the last time you took a vacation?"

"I go to that conference in San Jose every year," he protested.

On the other end of the videoconference, Ford mumbled something to someone in the background. A second later, Kitty leaned into view again and spoke over Ford's shoulder. "Matt, darling, going to a conference for work forty-five minutes from your house is not the same thing as going on vacation." Her gaze shifted as she redirected her gaze to Jonathon. "And you should get off his case. He deserves a break. Not everyone is as married to the company as you are. Thank goodness."

Kitty and Ford exchanged a look of intimacy that made Matt a little uncomfortable. He couldn't imagine what it would be like to share that kind of bond with someone. He, Ford and Jonathon were as close as brothers and had been since middle school. Hell, he liked them a hell of a lot more than his actual brother. Still, he couldn't help envying Ford's relationship with Kitty. They were close in a way he'd never been with another person. Except maybe Claire, and look how that had turned out.

Maybe some people just weren't meant to have that.

After a few more painless jabs from Ford about working too hard, Matt ended the conversation. Pretending to be friends to eschew gossip was one thing, but he was more than ready to take this "friendship" to the next level.

* * *

Claire lived in a quirky 1920s cottage on the south side of town. Long and narrow, it sat perched at the top of her steeply sloping lot. The previous owner had added meticulously terraced landscaping, which she tried to maintain. Like the other houses on her street, it was quaint. Even though the neighborhood was neither fancy nor particularly desirable, it was stable and quiet, with most of the residents being either older couples or young singles like herself. It was the kind of neighborhood where people turned off their porch lights at nine sharp and went to bed with their TV remotes or mystery novels not long after. No one ever rang a doorbell after ten.

So Claire had already showered and dressed for bed in her boxer shorts and tank top when Matt rang hers at ten-fifteen on a Tuesday night. When she spied his familiar form through the peephole, she very nearly went back to bed. Then as if sensing her ambivalence, he rang the bell again and called out, "Claire, the longer I'm out here, the more people are going to see me."

She flicked the dead bolt and swung open the door, but stood there, blocking his entrance. "I'm not letting you in, Matt. You're breaking your promise."

He didn't bother to pretend to misunderstand. "I'm tired of pretending we're just friends." With his hands shoved deep into his pockets and his voice practically pouting, he seemed like a little boy complaining because he'd lost his favorite toy. But there was nothing childlike about the heat in his eyes. Then he lowered his voice to a sensual caress. "I'm tired of playing games."

Her resolve wavered, but she tried to make her voice sound firm. "I have to be up early in the morning. I'm tired. It's too late."

God, she'd said a mouthful there. She was tired. Just

exhausted from the week of balancing work and trying to keep Matt occupied.

And it was too late. Not only too late at night but too late in her life. She, quite simply, felt too old to be doing this.

Still he braced his shoulder on the doorjamb and ducked his head as he smiled that roguish smile of his and something inside of her tightened.

"Come on, Claire." He snagged her hand with his own and toyed with it, running his thumb over the skin of her finger pads. "Just let me in."

His voice was low and soft, coaxing. His touch light and so seemingly innocent. Heat curled through her belly, making the sensitive flesh between her legs pulse with need.

A memory flashed through her mind, of him standing just like that, outside her college apartment, head ducked, smile shy, as he nervously asked her on their first date. He'd been so different twelve years ago. But then again, so had she.

She had run into him just that day in a coffee shop not far from campus. He, Ford and Jonathon had been sitting at a table in the corner, deep in discussion when she'd walked in. Her heart had started pounding the second she'd seen Matt.

A couple of years ahead of her at school, they'd always awed her a little. Ford had been the most popular guy in their class, able to charm any girl he'd wanted. Jonathon had been from a poor family, with a crappy home life. He got into a lot of fights, but Matt and Ford always backed him up. But Jonathon wasn't the kind of kid you felt sorry for. She'd known even then that he wouldn't be in Palo Verde forever. He just had that look in his eyes. Like he'd do anything to get out. She'd recognized it even as a kid because she'd felt that way herself.

But it had been Matt she'd always had a bit of a crush on. Even as a freshman in high school, when he'd been a senior. He'd been awkward, but so serious and intense. He too had clearly been destined for things greater than Palo Verde.

And when she'd seen him in that coffee shop near campus, her heart had started pounding so loudly she was sure everyone could hear it. He'd looked up, just as she'd walked past. Those whiskey-brown eyes had met hers and she'd felt like her insides had melted and might just slip out through the soles of her feet. He'd nodded and said hello. She'd barely been able to squeak a reply before hurrying to catch up with her friend.

She cursed herself the rest of the day for not stopping to talk. For being too afraid. Too nervous. Too awed by him. But then somehow, miraculously, he'd tracked her down. Shown up on the doorstep of her apartment to ask her out. And she'd let him in.

"Do you remember the first time you asked me out?" she surprised herself by asking.

His head came up, his expression a little wary. After a second, he straightened, as if he too were suddenly aware he'd been mimicking that posture. "I do," he said seriously.

Of course he did. It had also been the first time they'd had sex.

She hadn't been able to go out. Her very first college test had been the next day and she couldn't risk doing badly. If her grades dropped and she lost her scholarship, she couldn't afford more loans to make up the difference.

So instead of taking her out, he'd ordered pizza and stayed to help her study. And three hours later they'd ended up having sex on her sofa.

He'd been looking at her just like he was now, with all that intensity channeled toward her. It still made her knees go weak. But she was smart enough now to know better.

"At the time, I thought it was romantic, the way we couldn't keep our hands off each other." She tried to pull her hand away, but he didn't release her.

Instead, he moved closer, running his hand up her arm, saying nothing but subtly inching his way into her house. His gaze seemed glued to the progress of his hand, as was hers. Against her skin, his fingers were rough. His hand was at the crook of her elbow, his thumb tracing a circle on her skin.

She felt trapped by his touch. Somehow unable to get free of him. "Now, I just think I was an idiot."

He looked up at her now, eyebrows raised. "Not an idiot. Impetuous maybe. We both were."

She shook her head, finally finding the strength to pull away from him. But to do so, she had to retreat into her house and he followed, closing the door behind him. His presence instantly filled the narrow space of her living room. She wanted to retreat, but where could she go? Not to her cramped and tiny kitchen and certainly not to her bedroom. Her only choice was to face him down, here in the living room. It was an unlikely location for a showdown, with its carefully cultivated atmosphere of peaceful femininity. She felt like Sleeping Beauty facing down the dragon in her own castle. Now who was going to save her from the prince?

* * *

He could see her looking for a way out, but now that he'd breached her defenses, he didn't dare let her escape. He may never find a way back in.

Instead, he launched an all-out assault. Closing the distance between them, he cupped her jaw in his palm. Her hair was damp against his fingers, like she'd just taken a shower. Another woman might have played coy. Might have skittered away and acted shy. But not Claire.

Claire bumped up her chin and met his gaze full on. Clearly not quite comfortable having him in her home, but unwilling to back down from the challenge. That was his Claire in a nutshell. There wasn't a fight in the world she'd walk away from, even if she thought she couldn't win.

But tonight, this thing between them…it didn't have to be a battle. There didn't have to be a loser. They could both win. They could satisfy this crazy need that was eating them both alive. He just had to make her see that.

Matt didn't really have a way with words. Manipulating a conversation wasn't his strong suit, but Ford always said the most convincing arguments held a grain of truth. So that's where Matt started.

"We were both young," he said. "We're different people now. But here I am, still standing on your doorstep. Still just as desperate for you to let me into your life."

She laughed, a sound that was a little nervous while still laden with sexual promise.

"You find that funny?"

She bit down on her lower lip, her expression tinged with exasperation. "I find it funny that you think you're the one at the disadvantage."

"You never did get that, did you?" She tried to duck her head, but he nudged her chin back up. "You've always had all the power, Claire. I've always been completely at your mercy."

She looked a little awed by the prospect. And he could almost believe that she didn't see how much power she really had over him. She looked ready to argue. So he convinced her the only way he knew how. He showed her. He used something more powerful than mere words.

He pulled her to him and kissed her.

She tasted faintly of red wine and warm, cozy evenings curled up with a book. Her mouth was warm and pliant beneath his. A little surprised, a little resistant. As if she was still clinging to her protests.

As it had always been, kissing her was addictive. He wasn't able to stop. Was barely able to control his need, surging through him like a freight train. But he did control it at least until he felt the last of her resistance drift away.

Her hands plowed into his hair, clung to his shoulders, tugged at his clothes. And then she was pulling him backward, tiny steps toward a doorway at the far end of the room. He let her lead the way. Let her set the pace, because he was still afraid of moving too fast. Of letting loose his passion and overwhelming her.

Their clothing dropped away, his shirt hitting the living-room floor. Her tank top landing on top of it. His shoes toed off by the bedroom door. His jeans nudged down his hips and then off by her eager hands. Her boxers and panties in one quick swipe before he picked her up, wrapping her legs around his waist as he carried her the rest of the way to the bed. And then they were falling onto a pile of pillows and blankets, in a tangle of arms and heated passion.

He rose onto his elbow, staring down at her. Forcing himself to stop and catch his breath, to rein in his passion while he still held the shreds of his control. He waited there, her body trembling under his touch, her chest arching up to meet his, until her gaze met his. Until she looked at him, clearly and solidly.

He could see in her eyes that she hadn't yet accepted that this passion between them was bigger than either of them. He'd accepted it long ago. He'd known from that first night that she was meant for him. She'd been barely eighteen to his twenty-one. They'd never even been on a date and he'd known it.

Hell, looking back, he'd known it before he'd even graduated from high school. Kissing her now, breathing in the sweet, heady scent of her, he was struck with a memory from his senior year. It had been fall, the air just turning crisp, the scent of apples heavy in the air. He'd been sitting on the front steps of the school, waiting for Ford and Jonathon. She'd walked out the door and past him all the way to the sidewalk. Then she must have remembered something from inside, because she'd stopped, turned around and headed back up the stairs. She'd spotted him and stopped again. She'd stood there, four steps below him, so they were almost at eye level. Their eyes had met and neither had moved for the longest moment. As if time had literally stood still.

He'd wanted her instantly, but had been too terrified to even speak to her. He didn't know then what he knew now. But he'd known it when he kissed her that first time in college. He'd tried to forget it. He'd made himself block it out for twelve long years. But he'd always known it. She was his.

His love. His passion. His everything.

Nothing was more important. Not his work. Not FMJ. Not his friendship with Ford and Jonathon. Nothing.

And now, with that knowledge firmly in his brain, he gazed into her eyes as he thrust into her. Over and over. Telling her with his body what he wasn't yet ready to say again with words. *I love you. I'll always love you. I've always loved you.*

She didn't want to leave the safety of his embrace. And yet that was an illusion, wasn't it? As protected as she may feel in his arms, when it came to her heart, Matt was the most dangerous man she knew.

Resisting the pull of sleep and the magnetic draw of his presence, she pushed herself from the bed. A pair of jeans and a sweatshirt lay across the chair by her closet, and she quickly tugged them on. Obviously, her boxers and tank top didn't provide the kind of defenses she'd need.

Sleepily, he raised himself onto his elbows and watched her dress. "Where are you going?"

He looked ridiculously sexy like that, with the sheet tumbled down around his waist and his hair tousled. It would be so easy to climb back into the bed, curl up against his chest and let sleep claim her. They could make love again. She could wake up in his arms. Make him breakfast. And repeat everything the next time. And the next.

But how long could she keep that up? Always shoving aside the doubts that plagued her. Always waiting for the day he lost interest in her.

"I'm sorry, Matt," she muttered, apologizing as much to herself as to him. "I can't pretend anymore."

"Pretend what?"

"Pretend that this isn't going to end badly for me. Pretend that at some point in a few weeks or maybe months, you're not going to get bored with me—with this game you're playing—and you're going to walk out on me."

His gaze narrowed, he sat up then, plowing a hand through his hair before looping his arms around his raised knees. "You're so sure this is going to end."

"Yes." The bright gaze made her feel exposed and vulnerable. To distract herself, she began collecting his clothes and tossing each item to him. "Last time, at least, I had innocence and gullibility on my side. At least I could tell myself that I was young and stupid and didn't know any better. But I can't pretend anymore."

"What are you saying, Claire?" He ignored his jeans as they landed with a heavy thud at the foot of the bed. Even across the distance of the living room, she felt the force of his gaze on her like a touch. "You're not even going to give us a shot?"

"There is no us, though, is there?" She found one shoe but couldn't find the other. "What do we really have between us other than this powerful sexual pull?" Her heart thudded in her chest as she paused a second, clutching his shoe in her hands as she waited for an answer. And she hated that seed of hope that had taken root in her chest. That tiny part of her that wanted him to tell her that he really did love her. That the years that separated them were really just a misunderstanding. But when a heartbeat passed and then another, she finally spoke. "Great sex alone won't hack it. I can't just ignore all the other things between us. I can't pretend it's okay that you only want to take me to bed. That's not enough for me anymore." A burst of bitter laughter escaped as she heard herself say that aloud. "It never should have been enough in first place."

His jaw was tense, his gaze narrowed and shuttered, utterly unreadable. "And that's all it was for you? Just sex?"

"That was never all it was for me." She felt tears prickling at the back of her eyes. Turning her back to him, she scanned the floor. Dammit, where was that shoe? She pressed her finger to her temple. "But obviously it was only sex for you."

"Obviously."

She scrubbed away her tears. Placing the shoe on the ground near the foot of the bed, she began rifling through the pile of blankets that had been kicked to the floor. "And if we get involved again, you're just going to end up breaking my heart all over again."

"Breaking your heart? How did *I* break your heart?" She heard him throw off the sheet and rise from the bed, but she didn't let herself look at him while he pulled on his clothes. "You left me."

"I know. Yeah, sure, I left you, but—"

"There's no 'but' about it." He practically barked the words. "You. Left. Me. When it comes to breaking hearts, I didn't do squat. You walked away. And you made damn sure I wouldn't want to follow you when you did."

"Right." Her voice was bitter. "But when I left you, I didn't think it was forever."

"So you thought you'd be able to skewer me emotionally. Ride off with Mitch on the back of his motorcycle and come crawling back to me when you were done playing with some other guy?"

For a second she just stared at him, barely able to decipher his words. "Mitch?" And then she remembered.

The lie she'd told him when she'd left. The guy she'd invented to convince Matt she was serious about leaving. Just a name she'd thrown out from her mother's past. "No. There was no Mitch." She sat down on the floor with a thud, the search for the missing shoe abandoned, her arms full of blankets. "There was never anyone else."

"You said," he enunciated clearly, "you were leaving for another guy. For someone more fun. More adventurous. If you didn't go to New York with him, then where did you go?"

"How have you not figured that out?"

"Indulge me."

"I came home. I came back to Palo Verde." Back to the mess both their families had created. To the sister who needed her help, but resented it. To the grandparents who turned their backs on both of them. To a town ready to think the worst of her. And none of that had been as hard as watching from a distance as he moved on with his life as if she'd never been in it.

She looked up at him now, waiting for him to say something. His lips were pressed into a thin line, his expression grim.

"You were so desperate to get away from me, you had to invent reasons to leave."

"No. I was inventing reasons to make sure you didn't follow me." Suddenly, she realized she was shivering. She pulled one of the blankets around her shoulders and stood up. "That was back when I thought you actually cared enough to follow me. Back before I realized the truth. That guy I loved in college, he didn't really exist. He was just someone who said all the right things to get me into bed."

"You don't really believe that."

"I don't know what I believe now. But then? Yeah." She nodded, meeting his gaze head-on. "I really believed it then. Everything you did after I left only proved to me that you were just like the rest of them. You were just another Ballard who thought Caldiera girls were nothing more than white trash who could be slept with and discarded. For all I know, that's still what you believe."

What the hell was that supposed to mean?

But before Matt could even formulate the question, Claire left the bedroom. He followed her to the living room where she stood by the door. She may have looked fragile, standing there wrapped in a cuddly blanket, but the resolve written in the lines of her face warned him otherwise. "I'm sorry, Matt, I just can't do this anymore. I can't wait around for you to break my heart again. I want you to leave."

"I'm not—"

"I want you to leave town. Nobody needs you here complicating things."

Her words were like a knife in the gut. Brutal, painful. Potentially deadly. He snatched his shirt from the floor and pulled it over his head. Then propelled by some need he didn't understand, he stalked across the room and pulled her into his arms. He slid one hand into her hair, which was loose about her shoulders. The strands were slightly damp close to her head where her hair hadn't yet dried from her shower. The locks seemed to cling to his fingers.

At first she tensed against him, her hands wedged between them. But when he brought his mouth down to hers, her lips were soft and pliant. She smelled of shampoo and lavender soap and hot sex. After the briefest instant, she seemed to melt against him. The throw around her shoulders dropped to the floor. The last of her defenses falling away. The defiance in her eyes hadn't made it to her mouth yet. Intellectually, she may want him to go, but her body wasn't ready to say goodbye. Her hands yielded, stroking his chest, snaking up around his shoulders and into his hair.

Relief flooded him. Whatever else she seemed to think stood between them, at least they had this. They would always have this.

He kissed her long and hard. His tongue seeking hers over and over. He didn't even dare to lift his mouth, just plastered himself against her warmth and held on, secure in the knowledge that if he could just keep touching her, she wouldn't make him leave. All he had to do was never let go.

Then, as his mouth moved against hers, he tasted the poignant saltiness of tears. Her tears.

Forcing himself to pull back, he still didn't release her completely, but took in the sight of her. Eyes squeezed closed, lashes spiky, mouth damp and parted, lips red, cheeks streaked with tears.

Slowly, her eyes fluttered open. There was sorrow there, as well as an accusation.

"That just proves my point," she said softly. "Does it make you feel better knowing I can't resist you?"

He almost wished it did.

But he didn't want her to be unable to resist him. What he wanted was for her to need him as badly as he needed her. Not just in bed. But in her life.

Before he had a chance to admit that—before he even had a chance to think about whether he was ready to admit that—she pointed to the door. "Just go. It'll be easier on everyone."

"Easier on you maybe," he said. Because, dammit, it sure as hell was not going to be easier on him. Despite that, he left. Shoeless and barefoot, he stalked out into the night, far more miserable than he'd been when he arrived.

Nine

Matt didn't have the kind of relationship with his brother where he could go and ask Vic for advice. A therapist he'd once dated had suggested their parents fostered an unhealthy rivalry between them from a young age. He'd broken up with her about twenty minutes later.

He didn't need anyone to tell him that Vic was an ass and that no one in his family—not his former football player dad, not his social-climbing mom and certainly not his bully of a brother—had known what to do with a kid who was smarter than all of them combined.

Which was only one of the reasons why Matt hadn't stepped into the offices of Ballard Enterprises since his father's will had been read there five years ago. As he waited outside the office that had once belonged to his father and where his brother now worked, he almost wished he'd had the kind of brother he could go to for advice.

But he'd been about six when he accepted that he'd never have that kind of relationship with Vic. No. Six and a half. He'd been six and a half years old when he realized that Vic would always look out only for himself. Vic had dared Matt to dismantle the brand-new Macintosh computer their father had just bought. Matt still believed he could have put it back together, if only Vic hadn't called their parents and ratted him out.

Matt had known then that Vic would always screw him over if given half a chance. And so Matt hadn't given him one.

But now…well, now, he was pretty sure that at least part of whatever the hell was wrong between him and Claire had something to do with either Vic or their mother.

Since Claire had asked him to go—no, begged him, dammit—he didn't see that he had any choice but to leave. However, if his family had been giving her a hard time, he was certainly going to put a stop to it before going.

After keeping Matt waiting for over an hour, Rachel, Vic's anemic bombshell of a secretary, finally received a page from the phone, and told Matt that Vic could see him. She toddled over to the office door and held it open for Matt, her hip popped out suggestively and her eyelashes fluttering in a manner she no doubt thought attractive.

Matt barely gave her a second glance as he lowered himself to the wingback chair opposite the desk. The office hadn't changed much since their father's days as the head of Ballard Enterprises. The oak paneling, which had previously boasted a variety of framed photos of their father smiling next to different elected officials and celebrities, now held similar photos of Vic. One of the shelves on the bookcase had been emptied to house paraphernalia from Vic's career as a college football star, but other than that, everything looked about the same but twenty years older.

Even Vic, who Matt hadn't seen since the funeral—other than the night of the fundraiser—was starting to look much as their father had when they were boys. Shoulders broad, girth just a little too massive, jaw as square as a Neanderthal's.

As Matt walked into the room, Vic made a big show of being on a phone call on his Bluetooth headset. As if he were too important to waste the sixty seconds it took Matt to cross the antechamber.

After a few minutes of a conversation that Matt was pretty sure was about a fantasy football team, Vic hung up, stood and held his hand out across the desk. "How you doing, bro?"

Matt didn't even stand. "I need you to leave Claire alone."

Vic stood there a moment longer, his hand hanging in midair. Then he pulled it back, ran it over the side of his hair, smoothing down strands that weren't the least bit out of place. His smile widened, all congenial innocence. "I don't know what you mean."

"I'm leaving town." Matt leaned forward, bracing his elbows on his knees. "I got the impression from some of the things she's said, that you—or possibly our mother—sometimes give her a hard time."

"I don't know what—"

"It stops now." His tone brooked no argument.

Vic held up his hands in a gesture of benign innocence. "But I don't—"

Matt stood. "Now. I don't want you to talk to her. I don't want you to so much as step into her diner. And I want you to make sure Mother knows to do the same."

Finally, Vic dropped the facade. He studied Matt, his gaze calculating. "Man, she has really got you by the balls, doesn't she?"

"Vic, leave it alone."

But Vic wasn't smart enough to heed the warning in Matt's voice. "Don't get me wrong. I can see why. She is one tasty little piece of—"

Vic didn't get the chance to finish the thought. Something inside of Matt snapped. The repressed anger of a lifetime of dealing with his family's manipulative crap burst out. He rounded the desk and slammed his brother against the wall, pressing his forearm against Vic's throat. Vic's mouth flapped open as he gasped for breath, his gaze registering shock.

"You know what your mistake is, Vic? You've always assumed that because I'm smart, I'm not also tough. You picked on me my whole life, and I let it go, because it wasn't worth it to fight you. So you have no idea what I'm capable of." Matt felt the soft pliancy of his brother's throat. Felt the sharp bite of Vic's fingers clawing at his arm. And felt the satisfaction in knowing Vic wasn't strong enough to shake him off.

Finally, he stepped back, letting Vic go. Shaking out his arm, he said, "If you so much as look at her again. If you even breath in her direction, I will come back to town and I will crush you."

"You wouldn't." Vic's hands were at his throat, massaging the spot where Matt's forearm had been. "You couldn't."

"Ballard Enterprises barely supports you or Mom

anymore. For years now you've both been quietly selling off your shares to me to finance your lifestyle. I could own this company outright before you know it. And I would love to take it apart, piece by piece, and leave you with nothing. Don't be stupid and make it any more tempting than it already is."

"You wouldn't do that to your family."

Matt gave one last look at the office from which their father had ruled his little empire.

"You're not my family anymore." He turned his back on Vic, fully intending to walk out of the offices and never again set foot in the same room as his brother.

He took one last look back to see Vic hitching up his pants, his chest puffing out the way it used to just before he picked a fight with some kid too small to fight back.

"What, you think that Walstead kid is your family now?" Vic hurled the accusation. "You think they're going to want anything to do with you?"

Matt stopped and slowly turned to face his brother once again. "What was that?"

Vic's gaze narrowed, assessing Matt in that scheming, snaky way he had. Then one corner of his mouth curled up in a sneer. "She didn't tell you."

"She didn't tell me what?"

The sneer turned into a full belly laugh, the kind tinged with gleeful hatred. "If I were you, I'd go find Kyle Walstead and take a real good look at him."

Claire's house was within easy walking distance of Cutie Pies. Close enough to Main Street for the neighborhood to be aging and not quite popular. North of Main, most of the houses had been renovated into trendy showplaces, but the smaller bungalows in this neighborhood were still on the worn-down side. But her small house sat back from the road on a decent-size lot with a pine tree towering in the front yard. Half a dozen steps led up to the porch that stretched across the front of the house.

Matt had sat in his car outside her house a good half hour the previous evening after he'd walked out of her house, leaving her in tears. He hadn't ever thought to come back. But he needed to know just what the hell his brother had meant about Kyle Walstead.

Shelby Walstead had said Kyle hung out at Cutie Pies after school on Wednesdays. So Matt knew he couldn't go there to talk to Claire. He'd come to her house precisely because he wanted to avoid talking to the kid. Which made it very inconvenient that Kyle was there waiting on her porch when Matt pulled up.

He didn't look like much. The only other time Matt had seen him, through the plate-glass windows of Cutie Pies, Matt hadn't gotten that really good look his brother recommended. Now, as Matt crossed Claire's yard, he studied the boy. He was either young or scrawny for his age.

For a moment, Matt considered leaving all together. He had zip experience with kids. But whatever was up with Claire, this kid was in the middle of it.

The boy tensed as Matt moved up the steps. For a second, he frowned as if surprised, then he hopped to his feet, nervously rubbing his palms up and down the legs of his pants. He wore a baseball cap pulled low over his eyes, making it hard to see much of his face.

Matt paused at the bottom of the stairs and squinted up into the shade of the porch. "Hi. You're Shelby's boy."

The boy looked at Matt like he was an idiot, then gave

a tentative nod. "Yes, sir." He had his hands shoved deep into his pockets, his shoulders set in a defensive slouch. "You're that guy."

His tone made it obvious. *That guy* was an insult.

Matt wasn't good at gauging the age of kids, but he put this kid on the early side of his teens, maybe eleven or twelve, if he was small for his age. Just old enough to be distrustful of adults. There was something vaguely familiar about his posture. Matt could see a glimpse of himself in the kid's suspicious belligerence.

Unsure what else to say, Matt just nodded. "Yes. I guess I am that guy." He started up the steps. "You waiting for Claire, too?"

The boy backed up, as if trying to judge whether or not he dared to let Matt onto the porch with him. Finally, he edged to the far side of the steps and sat back down, his shoulder pressed snug against the wooden column. Matt lowered himself to the other side of the step, resting his elbows on his knees and giving the boy another furtive look. Maybe he was being an idiot, but if this kid was at the center of some big deep mystery, he sure didn't see it.

"I thought Claire said you hung out at Cutie Pies on Wednesday afternoons," Matt prodded.

"I do. But Aunt Claire called in sick today." Then he broke off, ducking his head. "I wanted to talk to her but she's not here now, so I thought—"

"Aunt Claire?" Matt interrupted the kid.

"Yeah."

Matt pinched the bridge of his nose, feeling like the conversation had suddenly gotten a lot more complicated. "I thought Claire's sister was named Courtney."

He considered it for about a second. He'd been sure that was the name of Claire's sister. Even if he'd remembered incorrectly, Shelby and Claire looked nothing alike. And Shelby was far too old to be Claire's younger sister. It just didn't add up.

When Matt looked back at him, the boy had pulled off his hat and was scrubbing a hand through his hair awkwardly.

"I'm adopted," the kid said. He didn't seem self-conscious about it, but instead gave Matt an odd assessing look as he added, "Aunt Claire is my real aunt."

It was the boy's tone that clued Matt. The way he said it so clearly, as if he were stating the obvious. As if Matt should have known something but was too stupid to see the truth in front of his eyes.

And then Matt finally got that good look at Kyle. The boy's features still had the softness of youth about them. The lines of his face still undefined. But the similarity to Claire was unmistakable. It was there in the jut of his jaw and the pointiness of his chin.

In fact, only his eyes differed. They were a unique shade of light brown. The exact same shade as Matt's.

Claire knew she was in trouble the moment she pulled up in front of her house and saw Kyle and Matt both sitting on her front porch. Her gut clenched in anxiety even as her heart leaped into her throat.

They looked so similar, both sitting with their elbows on their knees. Their postures similarly defensive. They were so alike, not just in looks, but in temperament, as well.

And here they were, face-to-face. She hadn't wanted them to ever meet, yet she felt the oddest sense of relief now that they finally had. Yet this had to be so hard on Kyle. Maybe she should have introduced them after all. In the end, trying to keep them apart had solved nothing.

Though her heart was pounding, she pulled slowly into the driveway. She clutched her keys as she climbed out, relishing the way they bit into her palm. The pain helped focus her thoughts and slow her breath.

Both Matt and Kyle stood as she approached. She walked up the steps, wrapped her arm around Kyle's shoulder and pulled him close. They stood, his back against her chest, facing down Matt together.

"I thought you said you were leaving town," she said. Which she knew was idiotic, but she couldn't think of anything else to say.

"You asked me to leave." His tone was hard and his gaze shifted from her to Kyle and back again. "That isn't the same thing as me saying I'd go."

She could practically read his thoughts. He knew now why she wanted him to go. More important, he *hadn't* known before. She was almost sure of it.

All this time, she'd believed he'd known about Kyle and just been ignoring him as all the other Ballards had. She'd been *so* sure. Now, for the life of her, she couldn't imagine why. His expression was so shocked, he couldn't possibly have known the truth.

To Kyle, she said, "Why don't you go wait in the car. I'll drive you home."

For a second, he looked ready to protest, but a glance in Matt's direction sent him scurrying. Smart kid. Matt's jaw was clenched tight. His fists, tighter. If it had been a humid day, tendrils of steam would have curled off of him.

As soon as Kyle yanked the car door shut, Matt spoke, "This is one conversation you can't put off by running away."

"I'm not running. And you don't really want to have this conversation with Kyle waiting in the car, do you?"

Her tone came off more defensive than she intended. Why was he angry with her?

She bumped up her chin. "What exactly do you think I'm going to do? It's not like I can leave town."

He leveled a steady gaze at her. "You're a runner, Claire. It's in your blood. Isn't that what you always said?"

"I may be a runner, but this is my home. I'll be right back."

She didn't give him a chance to respond, but marched down the drive and climbed into her car, clenching the steering wheel for a second before shoving the key in the ignition and starting the car. All the while, painfully aware of Matt standing on her porch, hands propped on his hips, eyes narrowed against the bright afternoon sun as he watched her pull away from the curb.

Her heart pounded in her chest as she navigated the streets of Palo Verde, turning out onto the highway and heading toward the new neighborhood on the edge of town where Kyle and his parents lived in a sprawling McMansion.

They were almost there before Kyle spoke, his voice small, his shoulders hunched. "He didn't know about me."

"No, he didn't."

Why hadn't she considered that possibility?

Why hadn't she just come out and demanded to know why he hadn't acknowledged Kyle? Then at least it would have been out in the open. It would have been a shock, but it wouldn't have seemed like she'd knowingly deceived him.

"Do you think…" Kyle said in stuttering starts. "Now that he knows, he might…I don't know…want to…" Kyle let the sentence drift off, his hopes too delicate to put into words.

"I don't know, honey."

Everyone in town knew who Kyle's father was. It had been obvious from about the time Kyle turned one, maybe earlier. Even Kyle knew it. But the Ballards never acknowledged him in any way. She alone knew how hurt Kyle was by their treatment.

He didn't dare mention to his parents that he longed for something from his father's side of the family. She didn't dare get Kyle's hopes up now.

"Matt doesn't have any kids in his life," she explained. "He might not know what to do with a kid, even if he wanted…" The excuse sounded lame, even to her. And she couldn't ignore her own part in this.

When she pulled up in front of Kyle's house, she turned in the seat to face him. "Matt isn't like the rest of the Ballards. He may want to have a relationship with you. But he might not. And even if he does, it might not be for a while. He just found out about you and he's probably mad no one told him before now."

Kyle stared straight ahead, his jaw set at a stubborn angle and his fingers clenching the legs of his jeans. "They should have told him."

"Yeah, they should have. But I should have also. I should have made sure he knew."

Kyle swiveled his head and looked at her, his gaze free of accusation. "Why didn't you?"

But she couldn't be so easy on herself. And *that* was the million-dollar question. How could she explain to an eleven-year-old what she barely understood herself?

For so long she'd resented Matt. She'd believed all the

things the media said about him. That he was a playboy. That he moved quickly from one relationship to the next. Maybe it had been easier that way. The man the media portrayed him as was easy to dismiss. It was all too easy to imagine *that* man not caring about a nephew he'd never met. It made it easier for her to pretend she hadn't missed out.

"You have to understand something, Kyle. If he doesn't want to see you, it may have more to do with how he feels about me and his family than how he feels about you."

After a long moment Kyle nodded and climbed out of the car. Then, almost as an afterthought, he leaned back down and looked through the window. "Aunt Claire, I don't want you to think that you're not enough."

Her throat closed off as she nodded. "I know, hon."

He'd said the same thing to her about his adoptive parents when he first suspected that Vic Ballard was his father. He'd come to ask her about it, explaining that he couldn't ask his parents, because he didn't want them to think they weren't enough.

She sat in her car, watching Kyle walk up the path and let himself into the house as long as she dared. Shelby's Prius sat in the driveway so Claire knew he wasn't going into an empty house. As much as he wished he was acknowledged by his father's family, he had two parents who loved him. That was a lot more than some people had. He'd be just fine, with or without Matt Ballard in his life. She just wished she could say the same for herself.

Matt was still waiting on her porch when she drove up to her house. Which was exactly what she expected, after all. She certainly didn't expect him to leave after meeting the kid who was his nephew for the first time.

She let him in through her front door. As soon as the door closed behind Matt, he grabbed her roughly by the arms.

"Why didn't you tell me I had a son?"

Ten

"What?" The word came out as a high-pitched squeal.

Matt had a son? What was he talking about?

"That boy is my son."

"Kyle?" she asked, trying to squirm out of Matt's grasp. *His* son?

"Don't lie to me," Matt ordered, giving her a shake. His eyes blazed with anger.

"I'm not. Kyle isn't yours!" she protested.

For a second Matt's hands tightened on her arms, then abruptly he released her, pushing her away from him. He turned away from her to scrub a hand over his close-cropped hair. When he spoke his voice was a low growl. "He has the Ballard eyes. And *your* chin. *Your* mouth."

Suddenly, Matt's meaning became clear.

"You think *I'm* Kyle's mother?"

"There's no point in denying it. The boy told me himself he's adopted."

"Kyle is adopted, but he isn't mine," she insisted. But before she could get any more of an explanation out, Matt whirled back around.

"He's obviously your son. Our son." He took a step toward her and then seemed to catch himself. He stopped in his tracks and shoved his hands deep in his pockets as if he were afraid to let himself touch her. "If you discovered you were pregnant after you left me, then you damn well should have told me before putting him up for adoption."

A bubble of panic rose in her throat. "*That's* what you've been imagining happened?"

"Do you deny it?"

"Yes, I do! Jeez." She wrapped her arms around her chest. "I can't believe *that's* the conclusion you came to. You meet Kyle, realize he happens to look a little bit like you. And then in the fifteen minutes it took me to drive Kyle to his house, you get 'Claire had a kid and put him up for adoption without telling me.'"

"It wasn't that big a leap. Obviously, you've forgotten how smart I am."

Completely flummoxed, she sputtered in indignation, unable to voice a denial vehement enough to convey her shock.

He must have taken her silence as assent, because he continued, his tone becoming more and more sharp. "Boy, that first morning when you said we weren't ready for the big talk yet, you weren't kidding, were you?"

"I certainly didn't mean this. That's for sure!" Anger propelled her to her feet.

"Are you saying you were never going to tell about Kyle?"

"What is it you want me say, Matt?"

"I want you to admit that Kyle is my son."

"Don't be ridiculous! I admit no such thing." She sucked in a deep breath, trying to calm her rattled nerves so she could think clearly.

But how could he think she'd done that?

"It didn't happen that way," she tried to explain.

"You must have known before you even left me that you were pregnant. You panicked. You knew then you didn't really love me, so you did what you always do. You ran."

Shocked recoiled through her. "Jesus, Matt. What kind of person do you think I am?"

He turned away as if unable to stand the sight of her. He stalked to the window and stood there, forearm braced against the window frame and stared out into the street. He didn't answer her question, but bit out each word of his response. "Just admit the truth."

Suddenly, her own anger boiled up past her shock and disbelief. Past her panic and confusion. She followed him to the window, stood beside him. She wanted to pound on his shoulder. Make him turn back to face her. Demand that he hear her out. "How could you think, even for a *minute,* that I'm capable of what you're describing?"

He didn't move except to turn his head to meet her gaze. His eyes were cold and distant. In his mind, he'd already convicted her. And that was what really pissed her off. He was so eager to believe badly of her. She had left him in college to save his future. She'd sacrificed herself for him. But instead of understanding any of that, instead of even giving her a chance to explain, he'd judged and convicted her on such cloudy evidence.

It was inconceivable to her that he thought she was

capable of such lies and deception. The idea that she might have put their child up for adoption was offensive.

It was a misunderstanding she could clear up with a few simple words, if he'd only let her get them out. But there was no way she was going to grovel and justify herself to him now.

"I've seen the kid, Claire. He's the perfect blend of you and me."

"And that's enough for you?" she asked with a sneer. "You've seen the proof with your own eyes and judged me guilty?"

"How could you think you could get away with this lie? Do you really think your protestations of innocence are going to sway me?" He turned to her again, taking her chin into his hand as if to prevent her from looking away. She didn't even flinch. "You think just because I was stupid enough to fall in love with you once that I'd fall for your lies again? Or maybe you thought just because we slept together I'd fallen in love with you already." He let go abruptly. "Well, guess what honey, I'll never be that stupid again."

"Well, you're acting pretty stupid, so maybe now's not the time to brag about your intelligence."

He ignored her retort. "Here's what I don't get. Why are you still arguing with me about this? You have to know that in this day and age I can have a judge subpoena a DNA sample from Kyle. I'll have proof by the end of the week that he's my son."

"And what exactly are you going to do with this 'proof'?" She made air quotes around the word *proof*. "Are you going to take Kyle away from the only family he's ever known?" Surprise flickered across his face. Obviously, he hadn't thought that far ahead. "You don't want a kid. Even if a court would—" She didn't finish the sentence. There was no point. It would never come to that. Because if Matt did do a DNA test, he'd learn he wasn't the father. "What good could possibly come of this?"

"I just want to hear you admit the truth."

"Well, then, we're at an impasse. What you really want is to hear me groveling and I refuse to do that. You get your subpoena and your DNA test and then we'll talk. Or better yet, you walk out of here and calm down. Sit down and do a little math, genius. Come back when you're ready to talk. Until then, get out of my house."

"Why are you back already? After yesterday, I thought you were determined to see every property in the county," Jonathon asked, looking up from his laptop as soon as Matt walked into the office.

Matt dropped his own computer bag on the table that served as his desk, suppressing a complaint. He wished he could avoid this conversation. He didn't want to talk about what had happened in Palo Verde. He didn't want to talk about Claire. What he wanted was to get back to work, where things made sense and problems were solvable.

Instead of answering Jonathon's question, he asked one of his own. "Wendy didn't talk to you?"

He'd called her from the car on the way home last night. Which was his other reason for coming in this morning. FMJ had resources that he alone did not. By himself, he wouldn't have the first idea of how to go about finding out if Kyle was his kid. However, Wendy could ferret out military secrets if she put her mind to it. He'd told her last night to find out everything there was to know about Kyle Walstead. And, to find Matt the name of the best family law lawyer in the state.

·In answer to Matt's question, Jonathon closed his laptop and rose from his seat to pour himself a cup of coffee. "She had her nose buried in work when I got in at six. She said something about you needing a lawyer. What exactly did you do in Palo Verde that you need a lawyer now? You didn't finally kill your brother, did you?"

"Very funny," Matt grumbled, only because he knew Jonathon was trying to rib an answer out of him. He didn't want Jonathon to know just exactly how unfunny this situation was. Instead of giving Jonathon more details, he concentrated on unpacking his computer bag, pulling out the pair of laptops he usually traveled with and hooking them up to the twenty-four-inch monitors he kept on his desk.

He clearly didn't do a decent job of hiding his emotions, because as Jonathon sat back down, he asked, "So how did it go in—"

"I don't want to talk about it."

"Then you didn't find any properties that looked—"

"No. I didn't. And unless you and Ford want to buy out my share of FMJ, I suggest you never again·talk about opening a branch there."

Jonathon pause, the mug halfway to his mouth. "Oookay."

Matt sank to his desk chair. Great. That was just super smooth. Jonathon would never guess something was wrong now. Matt knew he should probably apologize. But instead, he popped open his laptop and downloaded the mail that had come in overnight, including the revised manufacturing specs on the new wind turbines.

Which only made him think of Claire and the way she'd straddled him in that limo. Dammit.

He closed the specs, wishing he could do something that gave him more physical satisfaction than clicking a mouse. After a few minutes, he heard Jonathon open his own laptop and get back to work. Unfortunately, Matt's concentration was shot and he didn't make much progress. Finally, he stood, thinking maybe he'd be better off just walking over to the other building and seeing the thing in person. After all, he couldn't avoid the lab forever. Just because it was now drenched with memories of Claire, that didn't mean he couldn't face it. He now had plenty of memories of her at his house, too, and it wasn't like he was going to sell the place. No one had to know he couldn't sleep there anymore.

Before he reached the office door, Wendy knocked and opened it just wide enough to stick her head in. Acting unusually timid, she extended a manila folder. She looked at Jonathon, then ducked her head to whisper. "Here's that information you asked for. It's everything I could find quickly. If you need more, there's a guy in my building who's—" she sent a furtive look in Jonathon's direction "—a P.I. He specializes in this sort of thing. I can give him a call."

Obviously, she was trying to be discreet. Which he appreciated, but it still made him feel like a jerk. Ford and Jonathon had known everything about him since he was twelve. And it wasn't like he was going to keep this from them forever.

So as soon as Wendy had shut the door behind her, Matt crossed to stand a few feet from Jonathon's desk. He flipped open the folder and stared at the first page.

A copy of Kyle Walstead's birth certificate. Matt gave it only the briefest glance. In the spot where a father's name should have been listed, a single word was typed: *unknown*.

Matt flipped the page over before giving in to the urge to crumple it. The next several pages were obviously from the weekly paper in Palo Verde. There were several pictures of Kyle, one a close-up of his face accompanying an article about the battery-recycling program his Boy Scout troop had started. A couple of others were group shots with articles about his soccer team.

Matt felt a pang of regret so deep in his chest for a second he wondered if he was having a heart attack. Boy Scouts and soccer. Christ. Did it get any more all-American than that?

Matt looked at the pictures again. In the picture about the recycling program, Kyle looked much as he had the other day when Matt had met him on the porch: serious and thoughtful. Older than his eleven years. In the soccer picture, he was smiling, his arm around the shoulder of another kid, the group of boys holding a trophy between them.

That was the photo that gave Matt pause. What was he really doing here? Why even bother with the family lawyer? Was he really going to take the Walsteads to court? Or even Claire for that matter? Was he going to rip this kid's family apart all so he could have some sort of clumsy justice?

He was angry, yeah, but he couldn't imagine doing that.

Disgusted with the situation and with himself, he tossed the open file down on Jonathon's desk. "This is why I left Palo Verde early." He tapped his finger on the close-up picture of Kyle. "This is why I don't ever want to go back there again."

Jonathon slowly turned the folder around and stared at the picture. "Jesus, he looks just like you."

Matt scrubbed a hand over his hair and then met Jonathon's gaze. "Not just like me. He has Claire's chin."

Jonathon's gaze darted back to the photo. He let out a low whistle of disbelief. "She has a son she never told you about? Your son?"

"She put him up for adoption. So technically, Steven and Shelby Walstead have my son."

"Holy—" Jonathon cut off the expletive before it left his mouth. He shook his head. "I would not have pegged her for the type to do something like that."

"Yeah, me neither."

Unable to bear the glimmer of pity he saw on Jonathon's face, he turned away and walked over to the bank of windows along the wall. He propped his forearms against the glass and stared out sightlessly at the view of Palo Alto. The sprawl of office buildings that slowly bled into residential neighborhoods. The familiar red tile roofs of Stanford in the distance.

Normally, he loved this view. It made him feel like a god. How many men had accomplished all he had? How many men had made this much money by the age of thirty-three? Okay, yeah, so Ford and Jonathon both had. But they'd done it together. How many other men could say that?

His father, who had lorded over him his entire life, hadn't. And his brother certainly hadn't, either. Throughout his childhood, they'd treated him like a second-class citizen. His father had berated him. His brother had teased him. He'd been the scrawny geek. The object of ridicule.

Now that he owned one third of a billion-dollar company, no one made fun of him.

He didn't think about his relationship with his family very often. He wasn't prone to bouts of maudlin self-indulgence. But today, he couldn't help thinking how his relationship with his father had affected his relationship with Claire. When she'd left him, he'd stupidly—or perhaps pathetically—assumed it was his defect rather than hers. It had been all too believable to him that she didn't find him exciting enough. That he was too dull for her tastes. Why wouldn't she find him boring when his whole family did?

He'd moped around for weeks before his work at FMJ brought him back to the world. But even once he had more perspective he'd thought her fickle and unfeeling, but not devious.

Now, still reeling from the shock, all he could say was, "I never imagined her capable of doing something like this."

There was a long moment during which Jonathon said nothing. The only sound in the room was the faint shuffling of papers. Finally, Jonathon said, "Maybe she didn't."

Matt whirled to gape at Jonathon. "I can't believe you're defending her."

"I'm not." He held up his hands in a sign of innocence. "How closely did you look at this information?"

"What is there to look at? The kid looks just like me. And like Claire. Obviously, he's our son."

"It's not so obvious." Jonathon extended the birth certificate. "He was born in late February. You and Claire didn't start dating until October. He would have been extremely premature."

"Are you saying he's not my son?" Had Claire been

pregnant when they were dating? Wouldn't he have noticed something like that?

Since Matt hadn't taken the birth certificate, Jonathon returned to studying it. "I'm saying I don't think he's Claire's, either."

"What?"

"Claire is her given name, correct? Not a nickname. Because the name on the certificate isn't Claire Caldiera. It's Courtney."

"What?" This time, he snatched the paper from Jonathon's hand and studied it himself. The whole world seemed to telescope down to just him and the page.

Right there under Mother's Name was typed Courtney Caldiera.

"Claire's sister," he said. "Claire's younger sister."

Beside him, Jonathon let out another low whistle. This one filled with something like pity. "Claire's sister was what…two, three years younger than her. That would have made her—"

But Matt had already seen the Courtney's date of birth on the certificate and done the math. "Fifteen," he supplied. "She would have been fifteen when she got pregnant."

Matt felt as though the rug had been pulled out from under him…for the second time in as many days. He didn't think of himself as a particularly stubborn person, but he didn't like having his convictions blown all to hell.

Worse still was knowing how badly he'd misjudged Claire.

What if Claire was just exactly as sweet and loyal as he'd always thought she was? What if she hadn't lied to him about Kyle?

The girl he'd known then hadn't exactly seemed the

type to flake out on him and run off in the middle of her first semester of college. That had never fit with his image of her. He'd always assumed that he was just that bad a judge of character. But she *was* precisely the type of girl to drop out of school to return home to help out her pregnant younger sister.

That still didn't explain why she'd lied about it. But one thing was certain. He was tired of Claire jerking him around. This had to end now.

Eleven

Claire knew things were bad when she burned the third batch of doughnuts. All morning long, she'd tried to function. Tried to work past her malaise. But somehow the world seemed to be moving at double time while she was stuck in slow motion. Her short order cook, Jazz, handled the bulk of the morning crowd and eventually called Molly to come in early and take over waitressing.

Claire hid in the kitchen, trying to bake. And failing. How had it come to this? She could make doughnuts in her sleep. Jeez, since she had to get up at four to make them, most mornings she actually did make doughnuts in her sleep. So how had Matt messed her up so badly she couldn't even do this one simple thing?

Holding a burned doughnut in her hands, she felt her tears well up in her throat. She nearly laughed. After all that had happened, a doughnut was going to bring her down?

But instead of laughing, she leaned against the refrigerator and slowly sank to the floor, clutching the doughnut, struggling with her tears, hating the mess her life had become.

When Jazz found Claire still sitting there fifteen minutes later, the former marine slowly backed out of the kitchen. A few minutes later Molly came in. She sat down beside Claire so both of their backs were against the refrigerator. Molly linked their fingers and gave her hand a squeeze.

"Men are pigs," she muttered.

Molly's words sprouted a fresh batch of tears. "It's not Matt's fault."

"I meant Jazz!" Molly said fiercely. "After working here for four years, he finds you crying in the kitchen and all he does is come find me? Men are emotionally retarded."

Claire felt a hysterical burst of laughter bubbling up inside. "I don't blame him. I don't particularly want to be with me right now, either."

"You know what he said? He found me in the dining room and said, 'Dude, she burned the doughnuts and now she's crying.' When I asked why, he said, 'Huh?'" Molly gave her hand another squeeze. "Seriously. That's his big insight into the female heart. 'Huh?' Do you think they're all that stupid?"

This time, Claire really did laugh, the sound was part strangled exasperation and part humor. "Today? Yes. Today I really do think they're all that stupid."

Molly nodded. "Do you want to talk about it?"

Claire thought about it for a minute. She didn't want

to talk about Matt. Not even a little. She just shook her head.

Molly nodded, reaching across to take the charred doughnut from Claire's other hand. "Well, no one should have to deal with burned doughnuts and stupid men in one day. You should go home. Rewatch *The Notebook* or something."

"You know I never leave the diner before noon," Claire protested.

Molly ignored her. "Eat ice cream and dig around in your garden. Spoil yourself."

"Why didn't you tell me Kyle wasn't my son?"

Claire looked up to see Matt hovering on her front porch like an overzealous door-to-door salesman. The scene yesterday had been bad enough. The scene in the diner, somehow even worse. Now, she was wishing she'd stayed at work. Crying over doughnuts was better than facing Matt.

She'd barely slept last night, but instead had lain awake tossing and turning so much she'd felt like one of those hot dogs you see on a movie theater hot dog roaster, rotating on a spit, gravity causing it to flip every few seconds.

And now, he had to be here today, too? Why couldn't she get away from him?

Instead of answering his question, she walked past him and snarled, "I've had a really long day. So if you've just come here to harass me again, I'm warning you, I may call the cops and have you arrested." She paused, considering how that would go. Probably the police would show up, act all starstruck and ask for Matt's autograph instead of arresting him. Or maybe they'd just fawn over his Batmobile. "Or maybe I should zap you with my pepper spray myself."

The good news was, at least she didn't feel like crying anymore.

He stared at her, seemingly unimpressed by her exhaustion-induced rambling and asked a second time, "Why didn't you tell me Kyle wasn't my son?"

She slid her key into the dead bolt and turned it with a jerk. "I *did* tell you. Why didn't you listen?"

Her voice cracked as she hurled the accusation at him, making her sound pathetically desperate. How she still had any scraps of pride left, she didn't know, but apparently she did.

Forcing her gaze away from his, she hung her purse on the coat tree by the front door and slipped out of her jacket. Suddenly, she was aware of how she must look. Her attire was completely normal for her, and Matt had seen it countless times in the weeks he'd been here. Functional jeans and a bright pink T-shirt bearing the Cutie Pies logo. Her hair was pulled back in a ponytail that had been slick and serviceable this morning, but had no doubt frizzed into a halo. And she smelled like scorched chocolate.

He looked rumpled, but sexy in designer jeans and a long-sleeved shirt with the tail out. His clothes managed to look both ordinary and expensive all at the same time.

Just once she wished they could meet on even ground. But, of course, that wasn't possible. Between them, there could be no even ground. No equanimity.

They weren't equals. Not in position or wealth or power. He had all of it, she had none. Only a fool would forget that. Twice in her life she'd been very foolish, but she wouldn't be again.

He seemed to be waiting for her to say something. After a several moments of silence, he took a step toward her. "Claire, I'm sorry."

The words sounded torn from him. His expression a mixture of chagrin and self-deprecation.

Something about the way he was quietly fidgeting nearly made her chuckle. She knew she should be furious with him. And she was. Except just now she was too exhausted to muster the energy to blast him with the anger he deserved. She wasn't just tired physically, but emotionally, as well. She felt like all the fire had been extinguished from her soul.

So instead of yelling at him, instead of throwing his lame apology back in his face, she said, "God, you always hated admitting you were wrong about anything." Then, she was struck by a memory that really did make her laugh. "Remember the night we sat in that pizza place arguing for hours about which happened first, the French Revolution or the American Revolution. You thought the French Revolution happened first and nothing I said would convince you otherwise."

His cautious gaze shifted to amused. "That's not a mistake I would make now."

She shrugged. "Of course not. Twelve years ago it was a world without free WiFi in every coffee shop. Now your iPhone is never more than two feet away from you. You'd look up the facts before entering the argument. No need to ever be wrong again, right?"

Moving with deliberate slowness, he pulled his iPhone from his front pocket, placed it on the windowsill by the front door and walked to the opposite side of the room.

"The mistake I won't make again is not trusting your opinion. Besides, I never was very good at history."

More nervous laughter bubbled out. "Now that really is funny."

He slanted her a confused look. "It is?"

Another peal of uncontrolled laughter burst forth. "Don't you get it? You. Not good at history. Isn't that precisely the problem here? You, not understanding the history."

"I suppose so." He smiled, but there was no humor there.

The tight, tense gesture killed her inappropriate laughter. She just nodded.

He stalked closer to her. "Okay, Claire. I'll own to that. I *don't* understand the history between us. Why don't you explain it? Why don't you just tell me, once and for all, what really happened between us twelve years ago?"

"I guess I thought you'd figured it out yourself. That's why you came back, isn't it?"

He nodded, his expression suddenly fierce. "But I want to hear you say it."

"If you know Kyle wasn't mine…wasn't ours, then you know he's my sister's child."

"Yes."

"Then you've guessed the truth. That's why I dropped out of school. That's why I left the Bay Area. I never even wanted to go to New York. I was coming home to take care of Courtney."

"Why?"

She jerked her gaze to his. "Because she's my sister and she was fifteen and pregnant. I had to help her."

"Fine," he said, but his jaw was still set at that stubborn angle. "But why break up with me? Why not just explain what was going on? I would have helped."

The admission sounded torn from him. "I would have done anything for you."

"You think I didn't know that?" Emotion clogged her throat, making it almost impossible to speak. But she forced the words out. He deserved at least this. "That's why I *didn't* tell you. I was afraid you'd offer to come back home with me. And I was terrified I wouldn't be strong enough to tell you no. I couldn't let you leave Stanford. FMJ was just starting to take off. Jonathon and Ford needed you there. And you needed to be there with them."

"I could have—"

"I know." She cut him off. She simply couldn't bear to stand here and listen to all the things that he might have done to help her.

She stood up with a jerk and crossed the room, pacing away her energy. "I'm sure there are lots of things you could have done. If only I'd told you, you could have rescued my sister, lightened my burden, moved mountains and negotiated world peace. You think I haven't played that 'what if' game with myself a thousand times over the past decade? Probably ten thousand times is more like it."

He turned away, staring out her wide picture window into the street beyond her yard. His shoulders were slumped and his hands were shoved deep into his pockets, his mood impossible to read.

So she kept talking, voicing the concerns and doubts that had built up inside her for over a decade. "But the truth is, it's just as likely that you would have done everything in your power to help me and sacrificed your own future to save mine. Maybe you would have stood by and watched your friends go on to achieve phenomenal success and then eventually you would have resented me. Or worse, FMJ would have floundered without you. Then I would have ruined four lives instead of just one."

He spoke without looking over at her. "You should have told me. It should have been my decision to make."

"Maybe. But I know you, Matt." Saying that aloud tore at something inside her, because she wasn't nearly as confident in that statement as she wanted to be. At eighteen, she'd been sure she knew him at least as well as she knew herself. How many times over the past twelve years had she doubted that? Every time she read some bit of gossip linking his name to a model's she'd doubted it. And yet, the deepest moments at night, in the darkest, quietest parts of her soul, she'd still believed it. "At least, I know who you were then. If I'd told you, there wouldn't have been a decision to make. You would have done anything for me. You just said so yourself. Don't you see? I couldn't tell you. I couldn't risk it. I didn't do this to deceive you. I did it to protect you."

She heard the pleading quality of her voice. After all this time, he could still make her beg. Maybe he would have done anything for her, but the same was certainly true. It embarrassed her how much she wanted him to understand. Why was she so desperate? She didn't really believe that explaining herself might change things between them, did she?

Oh, God. She did.

It was there inside her. Buried under that need to make him understand. Hope.

She pushed it ruthlessly aside. She was done wanting things for herself.

"What exactly was leaving me supposed to protect me from?" His gaze seemed to burn a hole in her very

soul. She felt it deep in her bones. There was no hiding
from that look.

"I did it to protect you. Not because I didn't love you
enough, but because I loved you too much. I couldn't let
you leave FMJ."

"Okay, so you didn't want me to drop out of FMJ
to help you with your sister. But why not come back to
me? When Kyle was born in February. Why not come
back to me then?"

She averted her eyes, but he'd already seen the truth
in her gaze.

"Right," he said. "Those photos of me dancing with
Marena." He shook his head, a gesture part frustration
and part rueful. "God, you didn't trust me at all."

"It wasn't about trust. It took me years to get Courtney
on her feet."

"It shouldn't have been your job alone."

"Maybe not. But it was."

"Your grandparents—"

"They were why she was in that mess to begin with.
They insisted she tell them who the father was so they
could force him to marry her. She refused and they
kicked her out of the house. When she called me—"

Claire broke off, unable to finish the thought as she
relived that panic. Her sister had been on her own for
three nights before she broke down and called Claire.
She'd been hitchhiking to the Bay Area. At six months
pregnant.

Claire drew in a long slow breath, trying to fight
back the panic that still washed over her every time she
thought of all the things that could have happened to
her sister.

"Growing up in my grandparents' house, after my
mom left…well, I didn't have a lot of respect for them

to begin with. They'd never been able to control Mom when she was younger. I guess they thought they needed to be even stricter with us to make up for it. So it was always Courtney and me against the world. She was determined not to give in to them. I had no choice but to support her decision."

Matt's eyebrows were raised in silent question. As if he didn't want to interrupt her story, but also couldn't quite believe what she was telling him.

"Look, I know how it sounds," she said defensively. "She was fifteen. Too young to make that kind of decision on her own. Maybe she should have trusted them more. Maybe I should have. But you don't know what they were like. Rigid and unyielding." She met his gaze, hoping he'd see the truth of her words in her eyes. "They were going to force the father to marry her. Can you imagine? This guy who had slept with her and dumped her, this guy who let her get kicked out of her home and didn't do anything to help her. Can you imagine what it would have been like for her to *marry* him? I can't blame her for not telling them who he was. She didn't even tell me who the father was. But because she'd defied them, they wouldn't let her come home. Even after she'd had the baby. Not that I would have sent her to them anyway. Besides, by then, I'd already gone to my Aunt Doris and begged for a job."

She nearly cringed remembering how humiliating that had been. Doris had never gotten along with her sister, Claire's grandmother. So even though Claire grew up knowing they were related, she didn't have a real relationship with the other woman. Still, with a semester's worth of school loans coming due since she'd dropped out, a pregnant sister to take care of, and all of their mutual belongings crammed in the back of her ancient Toyota, she literally had nowhere else to turn.

Aunt Doris had been like a guardian angel. A gruff, cigarette-smoking, Scotch-drinking guardian angel who worked twelve-hour days and expected Claire to do the same.

"Even after Courtney had the baby," Claire continued, "there was always something to keep me here. She was just sixteen then. And she was behind in her schoolwork. Besides, I owed too much to my Aunt Doris to leave. She'd started to rely on me. Besides, by then you'd moved on. Way past me. There were models and movie starlets."

"Not that many," he protested.

"Really, because it seemed like legions of them. And here in Palo Verde, everything any of you did was big news. The whole town followed your every move like you were the Beatles or something. Every time I turned around, someone was talking about some new scandal or romance." She couldn't keep her resentment from her voice. "Look at it from my point of view, Matt. In my whole life, there'd never been a man I could count on. Until you. You were the one man I trusted. I loved you so much I forced myself to sacrifice my happiness for yours. I'd thought I'd broken your heart. But just a few weeks later, you'd moved on."

For a long moment he was quiet. Finally, he crossed the room and took her chin in his hand, forcing her to look up at him. "And it never occurred to you that I acted that way precisely because you had broken my heart?"

Her legs seemed to buckle underneath her and she had the curious sensation that her entire weight was supported by his gentle grasp of her chin combined with the sheer force of his gaze. She felt something blossom inside of her as that tiny kernel of hope grew. "It didn't."

But even as her hope grew, she felt it collapse under its own weight. What was the point in talking about what might have been? She could see in his gaze that there would be no forgiveness. No second chances.

"You should have trusted me," he said, the accusation sharp in his voice.

His words stung and she found herself revealing more of her resentment than she intended. "Well, I wasn't at a very trusting place in my life just then."

He just looked at her, his expression hard and unyielding. "How convenient for you that 'saving' me meant you didn't have to rely on anyone else. 'Saving' me meant you could make all the decisions and take none of the risks. You didn't have to trust me to help. You didn't have to trust me to make the right decision. The decision you expected me to make. You just sat back and enjoyed your own superiority."

"It wasn't like that!"

"Really, then what was it like? Because from over here, it sounds like you broke my heart and then judged me when I didn't grieve the way you expected me to. From here it sounds like you created this arbitrary test, you never told me the rules, but you were damn quick to judge me when I didn't pass it…"

Confusion washed over her, making her knees woozy and her head spin. Was he right? Had her big self-sacrificing gesture been nothing more than self-protection?

She tried to force her mind back to the girl she'd been twelve years ago. Tried to remember how she'd felt. But she couldn't even consider his accusations without being overcome by waves of anger.

She hurled his words at his back. "If you honestly think I should have trusted you under the circumstances, then you clearly haven't thought much about Kyle. Remember him? That kid you were so convinced was your son. Have you stopped to ask yourself why he looks so much like you? Because once you do, maybe you'll realize why I felt like I couldn't trust you with the truth."

He stopped then, hand on the doorknob, but he didn't turn at look her.

Since she had his attention, she asked, "Have you stopped to ask yourself who his father really is?"

Finally, he looked back over his shoulder. "Of course I have. I'm the genius, remember." Matt's lips curved in a smile as humorless as the conversation. "Kyle is my nephew. Vic is his father."

Twelve

Matt had almost made it to his car when Claire called out to stop him.

"What is your problem?"

He paused with his hand on the door handle and looked up at her. She stood on the top stair to her porch, hands on her hips, her jaw set at a defiant angle.

The pose was somehow classic Claire, all bristling defenses, standing alone. Just her against the world.

"I don't have a problem, Claire. I think it's your problem you should be worried about."

"My problem?" She stomped down the steps. "What's that supposed to mean?"

He was tired of all her protestations of innocence. He pushed himself away from the car and took a single step toward her, but then stopped. "Since I've been back, it didn't occur to you, not even once, to tell me about Kyle."

She threw up her hands in a gesture of confusion. "Why would it? I assumed you knew."

"And just how was I supposed to know, Claire?"

"Why wouldn't you know? Your mother knows, your brother certainly knows. Hell, even your father knew. It never even occurred to me that you didn't know."

"Well, I didn't." He didn't bother to hide the bitterness in his voice. He shoved a hand through his hair, but that did little to alleviate his frustration. "Christ, Claire, I feel like I could write a book about the things I didn't know about our relationship." He ticked the items off on his fingers. "I didn't know your sister got pregnant. I didn't know why you left. I didn't know my brother was the father. Or that I have a nephew the rest of my family pretends doesn't even exist."

He propped his hands on his hips, unable to do anything more than just shake his head. She didn't seem to have a response, so he asked the question that had been haunting him since he'd read Kyle's birth certificate. "Why wasn't Vic ever arrested? She was only fifteen. That's statutory rape. He should have been thrown in jail."

Her expression was a little sad. "He's a Ballard. Your family had money and power. If anyone ever seriously considered arresting him for it, I never heard about it. When Kyle was two, right before the statute of limitations ran out on the crime, the Walsteads asked me if I thought they should pursue it. I told them not to. What good could possibly come of it? By then, Courtney had graduated and moved away. And she was still too stubborn to admit it was wrong of Vic to sleep with her. She argues to this day that she was mature enough to make her own decisions even then."

"And so his crime had just gone unpunished?" He

forced out the question, even though the answer was obvious. When she didn't answer, he added, "I can't accept that."

"You have to, Matt. It's not your decision to make."

But it was his decision. The other day he'd thought his anger with his brother had reached its peak. But it was nothing to what he felt now. He really would dismantle Ballard Enterprises and he would do it with relish. He would destroy everything his brother held dear.

Still he had to ask, "Has Vic done this to any other girls?"

"No. Just Courtney." Then she ducked her head, looking thoughtful. "I wonder sometimes if he didn't really care about her, in some sick way. If that wasn't what fueled his interest in me." Then she shrugged. "But I don't know."

"I'm still going to destroy him," Matt muttered.

"Don't. Neither Courtney nor Kyle need you to avenge them."

"It's not about that."

"Then what is it about?" Her expression was baffled as if she really didn't get it. Hell, maybe she didn't.

"It's about you always trying to handle everything on your own."

Her chin jutted out even farther. "Hey, I handled things on my own because that's how I've always had to do it."

"No." He moved even closer, forcing her to look up at him. "You handle things on your own because you don't trust anyone else to help you." He studied her face, taking in every flicker of emotion, but he didn't see even a glimmer of understanding. "You talk about your sister's stubborn pride and you don't even see that you've got that same pride. Only worse."

"I don't—"

"You do." He almost laughed then, as the truth of that statement hit him full in the chest. "You always talk about being a runner, Claire. But you're not. You're a pusher. You push everyone away from you."

"I don't!" she said again, her voice cracking on the word, as if she didn't quite believe it.

"Yeah, Claire. That's exactly what you do." Suddenly, his anger dissipated. He took the final step toward her, stopping mere inches away. With fingers that almost trembled he brushed aside a lock of silken brown hair. "Think about it, Claire. You never even mentioned him to me."

"I thought you knew!"

"No. If you'd really thought I'd known, you would have been in my face, demanding to know why I hadn't acknowledged him. But instead, you avoided the subject altogether. You'd rather assume that I was a jerk who just wanted to get into your pants than deal with the possibility that I might actually be a decent guy. I guess it's easier for you that way."

He waited for her to deny it. Or try to explain it away. But she didn't.

She just stood there, struggling to hold back whatever accusation she wanted to hurl at him. The sight of her there, tugged at something deep inside of him. So fiercely independent. So afraid to ask for help and even more afraid to need it. He wanted nothing more than to be the person she relied on, but he was done running in circles for her. "Well, I'll make this real easy for you." He reached into his pocket and pulled out the ring he'd been carrying for days.

For a second, he held it, clenched in his hand, debating what to do with the damn thing. "I bought this the morning after that first date. I carried it around with me every day we were together in college. Even after you left I kept it. Stuck it in a box in the back of a drawer. I told myself I was keeping it because I never wanted to forget how lost I felt when you left. Now I think the truth is I kept it because I never got over you."

She looked from his hand to his eyes, her own filling with tears. "What is it?"

He opened his palm to reveal the engagement ring he'd bought all those years ago, the simple band of platinum and the square-cut loose stone that had fallen out of the setting. "When you left the first time, I threw it against the wall and it broke. It seemed fitting."

She reached out her hand, as if wanting to touch the ring. Before she could, he dropped the broken pieces at her feet. "Now I know why I never got it fixed. Some things are beyond repair."

Claire spent the next five days carrying Matt's ring in her pocket and waiting for another burned-doughnut incident. She kept waiting for the tears to sneak up on her. For her grief to ambush her when she least expected it. But the emotional breakdown never came.

Before she knew it, Wednesday had crept up on her and Kyle was sitting at the counter of Cutie Pies, his science textbook open on the bar beside him.

She walked out from the back, drying her hands on the dishcloth tucked into her apron strings. "Hey, kiddo," she said, trying to muster a smile for his sake.

"Hey, Aunt Claire!" Kyle's own smile was brighter than she'd expected.

"How's the homework going?" Chatting with Kyle, something inside of her loosened a little.

Maybe she'd lost Matt, but she still had Kyle and she still had Cutie Pies.

Kyle had been doing his homework with a yellow number two pencil and now he used the eraser to scratch a spot on his forehead. "It's slow. I've got this science project due Monday but I want to turn it in early so I can take the weekend off and just hang out with him, you know? But I just don't get mitosis."

But by the time Kyle was talking about the intricacies of cellular division, her brain was still stuck on his pronouns. "Him?" she asked.

Kyle went still, his pencil poised above his spiral notebook. "Ah, crap. I wasn't supposed to say anything, was I?"

"I don't know." She feigned innocence. "Say anything about what?"

Kyle didn't fall for it. He eyed her suspiciously. "About Matt coming for dinner this weekend. Mom didn't tell you, did she?"

"No," Claire admitted. "But it's good he's coming to dinner." To distract herself, she swiped Kyle's red plastic tumbler and refilled it with a scoop of ice and water. "Has he…um, been there a lot lately?"

She had to force herself to ask the question because part of her didn't really want to know that answer. Matt was right, of course, it had been easier to assume he knew about Kyle and had chosen to ignore the boy's existence. It was so much harder to deal with Matt's rejection knowing he really was the decent man she'd always wanted to love her.

"Nah." Kyle was looking at his textbook again. Studying a drawing of a kidney bean–shaped cell. "He came by last week. Had a big family meeting with Mom and Dad. They didn't even let me in the same room with him."

He flashed her a wry smile and for a second he looked so much like Matt, she felt like her heart was being squeezed through a straw.

"I guess," Kyle continued, "they didn't want me to get too excited in case it didn't go well. But they must have decided he wasn't going to be a bad influence or anything."

Claire couldn't help but return Kyle's smile, even though she could barely suck air into her lungs. "No." She forced out the word. "He's a good guy. I'm glad you'll get a chance to know him."

Kyle frowned and wedged his fist under his jaw. "If he's such a great guy, why aren't you with him?"

She could see him struggling, trying to balance his loyalty to her with his fascination with Matt. She leaned over, propping her own elbows on the counter across from him, so she and Kyle were at eye level.

"Hey, what happened between Matt and me has nothing to do with you, okay, kiddo? I don't want you to think you're being disloyal by being his friend. It's just as much my fault as it is his that things didn't work out."

Maybe more.

But there were some things she couldn't say aloud, not even to Kyle. Maybe especially not to Kyle.

"It's just..." Kyle let his words trail off as he stared at the chrome and pink tile behind the shake blender. He stuck his pencil eraser in his mouth and gave it a thoughtful chew. "Do you remember what you said to me when I used to ask about why my mom put me up for adoption and didn't want anything to do with me?"

"Yeah." She nodded slowly. She remembered the

conversation vividly. Kyle had been about five. The Walsteads had been so generous to let Claire be an active part of Kyle's life since he was a baby, but Courtney had never shown any interest in the son she'd given birth to. Three years earlier, Courtney had graduated from high school, moved off to Sacramento and never looked back. Claire had long ago made peace with the shallow relationship she now had with the sister for whom she'd done so much.

Kyle took a long gulp of his water, then turned his gnawing attention to the end of his straw. "You always told me that my birth mother leaving me didn't have anything to do with me. That it was all about her. And that it didn't mean there wouldn't be plenty of other people who wanted me in their lives."

"That is what I said." She put her hand over Kyle's so that he finally met her gaze. "You're not worried about Matt walking out on you once you get to know him, are you? Because if he says he wants to be with you, then you should believe that. He's a man of his word."

Kyle looked at her, those whiskey-brown eyes of his narrowed in confusion. "Then why didn't you believe him when he said he wanted to be with you?"

Claire straightened, sucking in a deep breath of shock. "I…I don't know." She pressed her hand to her belly, suddenly feeling woozy. It was a hell of a thing, having the rug jerked out from under you by a scrappy eleven-year-old boy.

Kyle shifted his shoulders, shrugging in a gesture that looked very much like Matt. "I just figured, if you thought I should trust him not to leave, shouldn't you?"

"But he did leave," she pointed out. And then immediately felt ridiculous for having this discussion with Kyle, who was only eleven and couldn't possibly understand the intricacies of adult relationships any more than he could mitosis.

But Kyle just tilted his head to the side and studied her. "Did he really leave? Maybe he just wanted you to be the one to chase after him for once."

Then again, Kyle was Matt's nephew. He was probably smarter than most kids his age. It certainly seemed that he was smarter than she was.

When Matt showed up at the Walsteads' house on Saturday, he found Claire sitting on the top step of their front porch, guarding their door like a Cerberus before the gates of hell. Her gaze was narrowed, her jaw clenched. He wouldn't have been surprised if she'd growled when he walked up the steps.

Her fierce expression was at odds with her appearance. For once, she was dressed in something other than jeans and a Cutie Pies T-shirt. It was only the second time he'd ever seen her in a dress. The first had been at the charity auction. That number had been an elaborate cocktail dress that had hung awkwardly on her, like she was unfamiliar with how to wear it. This—a simple floral number that nipped in at her waist before falling to drape over her knees in a froth of fabric—looked both feminine and comfortable. Like the dress had been made for her. Still, all that delicate femininity didn't lessen the effect of her determination.

He stopped at the bottom of the steps, holding the bottle of wine he'd brought in one hand and the gift for Kyle in a gift bag in the other. "If I'd known the Walsteads had a guard dog, I would have brought a raw steak instead. But here I am with just wine and gifts to buy my way into their affections."

Her gaze took in the items in each of his hands before returning to his face. "I don't think it's their affections you need to be worried about."

"Do the Walsteads know you're here, barring their door?"

Her lips twitched, as if she wanted to smile, but stopped herself. "Actually, I think they're listening at the door. I'm trying not to think about that."

"Let me guess then. You don't approve of my relationship with Kyle. You're here to warn me off."

She stood, gave her palms one quick swipe before catching herself and then tucked them behind her back. "Actually, I am here to give a warning. But not about them."

Surprised, he quirked an eyebrow. "No?"

"No." She pursed her lips, seeming to search for words. "The thing is, I consider the Walsteads family."

"So you are warning me to stay away."

"No, I'm just warning you that if you're going to be part of their family, then you're not going to be able to avoid me."

Slowly, she walked down the steps until she stood directly in front of him. Then she reached out and took the bottle of wine and the gift from his hands.

His heart started pounding, every instinct he had screaming at him to kiss her before she had a chance to escape. Screw his resolve to stay away. Forget all his intentions to excise her from his life and his heart once and for all. But he didn't move. Didn't even give himself the option to touch her, because he knew if he did, he'd never have the strength to stop.

After carefully setting the wine and the gift bag on

the step behind her, she stepped even closer, plastering her body against his.

She threaded her fingers through his hair and pulled his head down toward hers, stopping just shy of kissing him, so their lips were mere centimeters apart. So that when she spoke, he felt her breath against his lips.

"And I intend to make it very hard for you to walk away from me."

His hands still hung loose at his side and he had to clench his fists to keep from reaching for her. His blood pounded in his ears, his pulse thudding, his every nerve ending alive. "Why are you doing this, Claire?"

The one thing he needed more than her was answers. He needed to know this wasn't just a whim of hers. That she wasn't going to change her mind later and decide that he didn't live up to some mysterious standard that he didn't even know about.

She met his eyes, her gaze clear. "I'm doing this because I love you. Because I've always loved you. And because I'm guessing that you love me, too. If I'm not the love of your life, you've done a pretty crappy job of getting over me."

She rose up on her toes like she was going to kiss him, but pulled back just before her lips touched his.

"So what if you are the love of my life?"

Her lips curved into a smile. "Then I figure we're pretty lucky. Seeing as how we're engaged already."

"How do you see that?"

She extracted her left hand from his hair and held it up for him to see. Somehow the broken ring had been reassembled. Now, the metal of the ring wrapped around her finger, the two ends overlapping with the diamond wedged between them. "You gave me a ring."

"I dropped it at your feet. In pieces."

"But it was an engagement ring." She smiled smugly. "I'm keeping it. And I'm saying yes."

This time when she rose up on her toes, he closed the scant distance between them. Her lips were pliant beneath his. Her kiss full of love.

When he finally raised his mouth from hers, he took her hand in his and studied the ring. "How did you—"

"I brought it to the jewelers here in town. Martin designed a new band for it." She brought her other hand up to his cheek and paused until he met her gaze. "I asked him about this setting. He called it a tension setting. And he said he wasn't surprised it broke. Apparently, the man who first designed this style ring had the idea for the setting long before they had metal alloys strong enough to cradle the diamond. The rings were weak and prone to breaking. That first ring you bought me? The metal was too weak. It didn't stand a chance."

"And now?"

"Now, Martin made the new ring out of a titanium alloy that's super strong and it's not going to break."

"You sure?"

"Yes, I am." The look in her eyes told him she knew he was asking about more than the ring. "We're both stronger than we were twelve years ago."

He pulled back just far enough to say, "You need to know, I'm still going after Vic. I'm going to take control of Ballard Enterprises. I'm going to destroy him financially. Jonathon's already chomping at the bit to do it."

She nodded slowly, pressing her lips together. "I wish you wouldn't."

He nudged her chin up so she was looking him straight in the eye. "Courtney and Kyle may not need vengeance. But I do. He took you away from me. And he enjoyed doing it."

After a minute, she nodded again. And smiled slowly. "But you have me now."

They kissed again. A long, slow kiss full of the promises they both intended to keep. Whatever doubts he might have had dissolved under the strength of her touch.

When he finally lifted his mouth from hers, she socked him in the arm.

"What was that for?" he asked, rubbing his arm.

"That was for leaving me for a week." She frowned, her brow furrowing in question. "Were you really going to walk away? What if I hadn't come after you?"

He just smiled. "I think you just needed the time to figure out that you needed to come after me."

"I think I can live with that." She wrapped her arm around his waist and rested her head against his chest. "So what do we do now?"

"Now, we go have dinner with our family."

* * * * *

Silhouette *Desire*

COMING NEXT MONTH

Available December 7, 2010

REQUEST YOUR FREE BOOKS!

2 FREE NOVELS PLUS 2 FREE GIFTS!

Passionate, Powerful, Provocative!

YES! Please send me 2 FREE Silhouette Desire® novels and my 2 FREE gifts (gifts are worth about $10). After receiving them, if I don't wish to receive any more books, I can return the shipping statement marked "cancel." If I don't cancel, I will receive 6 brand-new novels every month and be billed just $4.05 per book in the U.S. or $4.74 per book in Canada. That's a saving of at least 15% off the cover price! It's quite a bargain! Shipping and handling is just 50¢ per book.* I understand that accepting the 2 free books and gifts places me under no obligation to buy anything. I can always return a shipment and cancel at any time. Even if I never buy another book, the two free books and gifts are mine to keep forever.

225/326 SDN E5QG

Name	(PLEASE PRINT)

Address	Apt. #

City	State/Prov.	Zip/Postal Code

Signature (if under 18, a parent or guardian must sign)

Mail to the **Silhouette Reader Service:**

IN U.S.A.: P.O. Box 1867, Buffalo, NY 14240-1867
IN CANADA: P.O. Box 609, Fort Erie, Ontario L2A 5X3

Not valid for current subscribers to Silhouette Desire books.

**Want to try two free books from another line?
Call 1-800-873-8635 or visit www.morefreebooks.com.**

* Terms and prices subject to change without notice. Prices do not include applicable taxes. N.Y. residents add applicable sales tax. Canadian residents will be charged applicable provincial taxes and GST. Offer not valid in Quebec. This offer is limited to one order per household. All orders subject to approval. Credit or debit balances in a customer's account(s) may be offset by any other outstanding balance owed by or to the customer. Please allow 4 to 6 weeks for delivery. Offer available while quantities last.

Your Privacy: Silhouette Books is committed to protecting your privacy. Our Privacy Policy is available online at www.eHarlequin.com or upon request from the Reader Service. From time to time we make our lists of customers available to reputable third parties who may have a product or service of interest to you. If you would prefer we not share your name and address, please check here. ☐

Help us get it right—We strive for accurate, respectful and relevant communications. To clarify or modify your communication preferences, visit us at www.ReaderService.com/consumerchoice.

SDES10R

HARLEQUIN®

A Romance

FOR EVERY MOOD™

Spotlight on

Classic

Quintessential, modern love stories
that are romance at its finest.

See the next page
to enjoy a sneak peek from
the Harlequin® Romance series.

CATCLASSHR10

*See below for a sneak peek from our classic
Harlequin® Romance® line.*

Introducing DADDY BY CHRISTMAS by Patricia Thayer.

MIA caught sight of Jarrett when he walked into the open lobby. It was hard not to notice the man. In a charcoal business suit with a crisp white shirt and striped tie covered by a dark trench coat, he looked more Wall Street than small-town Colorado.

Mia couldn't blame him for keeping his distance. He was probably tired of taking care of her.

Besides, why would a man like Jarrett McKane be interested in her? Why would he want to take on a woman expecting a baby? Yet he'd done so many things for her. He'd been there when she'd needed him most. How could she not care about a man like that?

Heart pounding in her ears, she walked up behind him. Jarrett turned to face her. "Did you get enough sleep last night?"

"Yes, thanks to you," she said, wondering if he'd thought about their kiss. Her gaze went to his mouth, then she quickly glanced away. "And thank you for not bringing up my meltdown."

Jarrett couldn't stop looking at Mia. Blue was definitely her color, bringing out the richness of her eyes.

"What meltdown?" he said, trying hard to focus on what she was saying. "You were just exhausted from lack of sleep and worried about your baby."

He couldn't help remembering how, during the night, he'd kept going in to watch her sleep. How strange was that? "I hope you got enough rest."

She nodded. "Plenty. And you're a good neighbor for

coming to my rescue."

He tensed. Neighbor? *What neighbor kisses you like I did?* "That's me, just the full-service landlord," he said, trying to keep the sarcasm out of his voice. He started to leave, but she put her hand on his arm.

"Jarrett, what I meant was you went beyond helping me." Her eyes searched his face. "I've asked far too much of you."

"Did you hear me complain?"

She shook her head. "You should. I feel like I've taken advantage."

"Like I said, I haven't minded."

"And I'm grateful for everything…"

Grasping her hand on his arm, Jarrett leaned forward. The memory of last night's kiss had him aching for another. "I didn't do it for your gratitude, Mia."

Gorgeous tycoon Jarrett McKane has never believed in Christmas—but he can't help being drawn to soon-to-be-mom Mia Saunders! Christmases past were spent alone…and now Jarrett may just have a fairy-tale ending for all his Christmases future!

Available December 2010, only from Harlequin® Romance®.

Silhouette *Desire*

USA TODAY bestselling authors

MAUREEN CHILD

and

SANDRA HYATT

UNDER THE MILLIONAIRE'S MISTLETOE

Just when these leading men thought they had it all figured out, they quickly learn their hearts have made other plans. Two passionate stories about love, longing and the infinite possibilities of kissing under the mistletoe.

Available December wherever you buy books.

Always Powerful, Passionate and Provocative.

Visit Silhouette Books at www.eHarlequin.com

SD73069

HARLEQUIN *Presents*

Bestselling Harlequin Presents® author

Julia James

brings you her most powerful book yet…

FORBIDDEN OR FOR BEDDING?

The shamed mistress…

Guy de Rochemont's name is a byword for wealth
and power—and now his duty is to wed.

Alexa Harcourt knows she can never be anything
more than *The de Rochemont Mistress*.

But Alexa—the one woman Guy wants—is also
the one woman whose reputation
forbids him to take her as his wife….

Available from Harlequin Presents
December 2010

www.eHarlequin.com

HP12960